Books by James Litherland

The Slowpocalypse Series

Critical Contingencies
Threat Multiplication
Compromised Inside
Peripheral Encounters
Political Homicide

The Watchbearers Series

Millennium Crash
Centenary Separation
Uncertain Murder
Prohibited Activities
Temporal Entanglement

The Miraibanashi Series

Code of the Kyoushi
Enemies of the Batsu
Endurance of the Free

For more information, please visit
www.OutpostStories.com

MILLENNIUM
CRASH

DEDICATION

To God be the Glory

(and all criticism should be directed at the author.)

MILLENNIUM CRASH

JAMES LITHERLAND

Outpost Stories

Disclaimer: As should be obvious, this book is a complete work of fiction. Any resemblance to real persons, places, or things is entirely coincidental.

ISBN-13: 978-1-946273-11-6

Cover design by James Litherland

Contents

Contents

Chapter 1

Two Crashes in Two Thousand

June 30th, 2000 Midtown Manhattan

ANYA kept her eyes open as reality rapidly reassembled around her—a concrete curb beneath her feet, the back and front ends of two taxicabs parked on the asphalt ahead of her—and about thirty meters in front of her stood the tall, slim, white-haired form of Professor John. He had been standing right beside her the previous moment.

In the few seconds it took to begin processing the new surroundings that were taking shape, Anya felt a vague sense of panic racing up her spine, an anxiety she didn't understand. Her instinct forced her to shout.

"Professor!"

Chapter 1

Anya watched as he turned toward her, confusion and disorientation plain on his face. While her brain still grasped at the nature of the jeopardy, the sound of tires screeching intruded upon everything, and a large black vehicle slammed into view—and into the professor. Reality crashed upon Anya with a vengeance.

Suddenly her feet were free, and she dashed between the cabs and into the street, head swiveling in every direction as horns honked all around her. She saw John lying awkward across the back windshield of another cab down the road. The SUV had braked hard as it hit him, propelling the professor into the rear of the taxi, which had also screeched to a halt.

Anya darted through the newly created parking lot to help John. Shouted swear words swelled into the continuing cacophony of car horns blasting, the overwhelming noise pressing upon her still struggling senses. The transition from the sterile, quiet conference room of a moment ago to this raging sea of stimulation was a bad jolt. The fall from a feeling of excitement for their journey to this horror deeply jarred her.

But she was adapting quick to the new environment. Even before she reached the sprawled figure of the professor, she'd begun to suspect it was hopeless. Up close, neither the blood nor the jagged bone poking out of his thigh disturbed her. She'd seen so much worse when she'd been a nurse. What made Anya's stomach turn over with incipient nausea was trying to digest the fact of John's death, the sudden and violent loss of her beloved mentor.

She wanted to freeze, to simply shut down. The whole project stood in shambles before it had even started. Her old training took over though, and the urgency of the situation prodded her into action.

She checked his watch. It'd been broken, likely shattered beyond any hope of repair like the professor himself. She fought back the tears. She didn't have time to worry about the destroyed device but slid the watch off his wrist and into her pocket without hesitation. She couldn't just leave it.

Anya didn't want to leave the professor either, but she had no choice. She looked up and around then and realized a large crowd had gathered, staring at her. They probably thought she was robbing John's body. Several shouted, others pointed, and some made gestures presumably rude—but no one tried to impede her flight as she ran from the street, diving heedlessly into that crowd. Something else had already attracted their attention away from her.

At first she couldn't fathom the lack of familiar faces—she had scanned the sea of those around her and kept looking as she passed through the people standing there. But she'd recognized no one. She'd not only lost the professor, she'd lost them all.

Turner and Nye, at least, had been standing less than a meter away when they'd all Traveled. Anya stumbled along the sidewalk, searching. *Where are they now?*

Anya herself had been standing right at John's shoulder—almost touching—and he'd materialized quite a distance from her. A fatal separation. The others must have been similarly scattered, and Anya needed to focus on finding them. They could be in all kinds of trouble themselves.

Her mind was spinning as she walked on, trying to think. She couldn't deal with all the implications of the professor's death and the destruction of his watch—not now. The critical thing was to regroup. Then they could deal with the rest. Together.

She continued to move away from the point of arrival, the scene of the accident. She had assumed the contemporary authorities would be en route— she could not afford to deal with them, not without identification. She'd have to rely on Turner and Nye having the sense to search for her.

Anya almost stopped dead in her tracks. She'd believed she had kept her wits about her, but clearly they were still scrambled. Worried that she hadn't put enough distance between herself and the scene, she waited until she'd rounded a corner and walked down another half block before she ducked into a dim recess to check her watch.

She took several deep breaths to calm herself. Only then did she lift her head and notice the actual city around her, great towering structures crammed onto this small island and thrusting so far up into the sky as to drape almost everything in shadows. *What a sight.* To think that humanity had once built such magnificent enclaves. *No wonder.*

Anya sighed and shook herself, bringing her focus back to the matter at hand. Digital watches with varied functions were supposed to be ubiquitous in this time, so she'd no concern about drawing undue attention by activating the locator application.

The screen didn't show any blips to indicate another device in range, but a blinking red bar on the right edge showed the direction of her nearest helper. *East.* At least it *should* be one of hers.

Hopefully the other research leaders had kept their heads sufficiently to be rounding up their own charges already. Or vice versa. At least they appeared to have all landed in the same time period. This geographical separation, devastating as it had been, at least for the professor, was a minor irritation compared to the disaster it would have been if they'd become lost in time.

Anya checked her watch once more, confirming they had arrived *when* they were supposed to. This *was* the summer of two thousand and the transition from the second to the third millennium. When so

<u>much had changed</u>. Then she left the alcove and be-gan tracking down her misplaced helpers.

As Anya stalked the closest of her fellow Travel-ers, she kept a close eye on the locator screen while trying to do the math in her head. Hard for a histo-rian perhaps, but she'd had plenty of practice when she was a nurse. The professor had been mere cen-timeters from her when they'd left, but he had come through tens of meters distant. And the rest?

There must be an algorithm that would account for the spatial dispersion. But she couldn't calculate based on an unknown equation—without more data points, she didn't even know if the progression was arithmetic or exponential. What she could and did understand was that they were separated by a con-siderable distance in a giant metropolis in a foreign time. And they might be trapped here.

The research leaders' ability to Travel was lim-ited, certainly. Even once Anya had found the rest of her team and reunited with the other teams, they couldn't dare make the attempt until they had some understanding of the strange and unexpected effect that had separated them. And returning home had become problematic as well.

Two long blocks of wading through the streams of busy pedestrians and she finally saw a blip on the screen. She eased her pace and considered the re-sults. As one of the helpers registered ahead of her, the indicator light began blinking to show the direction of the nearest device beyond her range. *South.*

Anya was momentarily tempted to go traipsing after that one, since the blip on her screen remained stationary, but a pigeon in the hand was tastier than one in the sky. And once she'd found another Traveler she would no longer be alone.

She grew irritated as her closest helper continued to stay wherever they were instead of coming to meet her. She could imagine different explanations for that, depending on which of her helpers she was tracking—when she crossed over to the next block and saw the small coffee shop snuggled into the corner of the first floor of the building, she suspected who she was about to find. *Nye.*

Indeed, as Anya eased her way into the crowded space, she spotted her helper sitting on a stool at the counter with a look of rapture on her face. It must have been the aroma or the place itself, since none of them yet had any funds for purchasing anything. That included a simple cup of coffee.

The professor had carried some contemporary cash on him from his previous trips, but he hadn't supposed his team leaders would have any immediate need for funds—and Anya had not considered taking the wallet off his body. Now getting ahold of some of their money had become an urgent matter if they wanted to eat. *I'm already getting peckish.*

7

Anya gritted her teeth as she waved, beckoning Nye to follow her out, away from the lure of caffeine and back outside. The girl with her big round glasses and straight brown hair and bangs hanging down across her forehead pouted. But at least she obeyed her leader.

Once out in the open, her mouth popped wide again as she gazed around her in wonder. "It's all so incredible. To see this city at its height."

Anya sighed. "You'll have plenty of opportunity to soak it all up. Right now we have more pressing problems."

"But it's so very different from digging through the ruins. The city's brimming with life. Teeming." It sounded as if she were already writing her dissertation in her head.

Anya grabbed the woman's wrist and pulled her along. "Come on, now. We've got to find Turner." That should get Nye moving.

Unfortunately, the girl did turn her attention to what her leader had been saying. "But where is the professor? Shouldn't he be here with us?"

Anya clenched her jaw to force back the tears, but her eyes welled up all the same. Thankfully Nye was trailing behind her and couldn't see. "You don't worry about the professor." This wasn't the time to try to deal with his death. "We must concern ourselves with locating the others."

Nye had to ask more questions though. "What happened? Why were none of the rest around when I came through?"

Anya shook her head. "I don't know. They were supposed to have tested everything so no problems would crop up when we actually Traveled."

"Machines always mess up. Computers are the worst."

Anya sighed and glanced over her shoulder at the girl. "What about the people who construct the machines? Program the computers?"

"Of course people fail. That's no excuse."

Anya almost smiled. "Well, I wish someone had considered more possibilities when they coded the locator apps. For one thing, they only indicate the eight compass directions, and the screen shows just the one plane."

"What do you mean?" Anya could hear the confusion in Nye's voice. "What's wrong with that?"

Anya shook her head. She wondered how Nye could be so jaded and yet so unpractical at the same time. "Look up, Nye."

She didn't look behind her, but nonetheless she could feel Nye craning her neck to gaze at the sky overhead. "It's strange to see so much sky blocked out by buildings."

Anya couldn't hold back a smile this time. "It's those buildings you ought to be looking at, Nye. I know you're used to seeing them as crushed mounds beneath you, but try seeing them as they are now." She shouldn't have to be telling Nye this. She wondered how an archaeologist could manage without using their imagination.

Anya explained. "Maybe you failed to study how the Traveling works, Nye." *Or how it's supposed to work.* "But it's possible to land above ground level, if there's something solid to land on. So Turner, or any of the others, could have arrived on any floor of one of these buildings you see."

"Oh." The wheels in Nye's brain must have been turning by now, thinking things through. The woman was smart enough when she made the effort, and she'd likely suffered from the same initial disorientation as Anya and the professor. Though Nye did tend to get lost in her own head anyway.

Anya checked her watch to make sure they were still moving in the right direction. "Actually, seeing how much is above ground here, chances are several of us might have materialized on some floor of one of these buildings. You didn't, did you?"

Nye had begun walking faster, matching Anya's own pace. "No. I arrived right outside that coffee shop. I would have thought it was my prayer being answered except I didn't have any money for a cup of coffee. But the aroma was amazing. That's why I went in, to enjoy the sights and the smell."

Anya nodded to herself. *Of course.* "So despite the probabilities, that's three of us that arrived outdoors."

"Three?" When Anya didn't respond, Nye continued, "Doesn't that argue that the rest of them will have come through outside as well?"

"Maybe." *Not necessarily.* "There's likely a bias in favor of ground level entry, and perhaps against arriving on the inside of a structure." Anya did not want to discuss time-travel mechanics or why landing at street level wasn't necessarily a good thing. "The point is, if any of the others *are* in one of these aptly named skyscrapers, our locator apps won't be much help since they can't indicate up or down." So determining what floor someone was on would be a problem. *But I have an idea about that.*

Nye shook her head. "But wouldn't anyone who arrived on the twentieth floor, for example, just go right to the ground floor. Then they'd start searching—everyone would be searching for each other on the same level."

It would be nice to think so. "You didn't start looking for me at all, Nye."

"I knew someone would find me. If I just stayed put. And anyway, I wanted to get started with my research."

"Coffee?" Anya shook her head. "And if you *had* landed on the twentieth floor?"

Nye's grin was fleeting. "Come to think of it, I believe a lot of the workplaces of this time had free coffee available for employees and customers." Her tone was wistful. "I might've actually gotten a cup."

Anya sighed as she envisioned Nye working her way down each floor in search of a caffeine fix. Then she noticed the directional bar on her locator swing back to the east as they passed one of the skyscrapers. *Turner must be inside.*

She stopped and stared up at the imposing sight before her. "Well, unless he's just standing around on the ground floor waiting to be found, like you—we'll see how this works."

Nye looked up the tower of gleaming windows. "Turner's in there?"

"Appears to be. Now to try and find him." The great revolving glass doors of the entrance intimidated Anya, but she wasn't going to let that stop her. She grabbed Nye's wrist again, staring at the doors for a long moment. To make sure. "Stay right with me." And she plunged them both into the building.

Inside, a vast lobby with marble floors made the place seem huge, despite the walls and ceiling. And everyone around them seemed to know where they were going. A uniformed guard stood around casually as the throngs of people streamed around him, and Anya briefly considered asking him for help. *I can always come back.*

First they would try to find Turner on their own, though Anya wouldn't expect that to be simple. She didn't expect anything to be easy anymore. Indeed, since her locator app still showed a direction rather than indicating Turner with a blip, the man had to be outside the range of the field, which was roughly a hundred meters.

Since he had to be farther away than that and in a big commercial building like this each story would be around five meters, they should find Turner on the twentieth floor or higher. Now she could put her idea to the test. If she observed the locator screen as they moved upward and noted at what point Turner became a blip, she ought to be able to roughly estimate how many floors above he could be found. *If he stays in one place.*

Anya walked straight to the middle of the lobby to a pedestal displaying a directory describing what was on each floor, dragging Nye along behind her. She noted there were forty-four floors in all. And she snapped a picture of it with her watch for future reference, because she was sick of being unprepared when everything kept going wrong.

Now the question was how best to get to the upper floors. With at least twenty floors to climb, she discounted the stairs and headed for the far side of the lobby where a long row of elevators stood. Normally such conveniences were for the sick or infirm, but here everyone seemed to be using them. It made sense, of course, with forty-four floors. But she saw there was a staircase in each corner on either side of those elevators, so some people had to be fit enough for the climb. *I am, but I don't have the time.*

"Come on, Nye." Anya kept a firm grip on the woman's wrist. With all these people moving every which way, she wouldn't risk losing the one person she'd managed to find so far.

They headed straight for the elevators, and Nye started to dive into the first open car, but Anya held her back. "Look at the numbers, Nye." Above each pair of doors were signs indicating which floors they went to. "Turner must be at least above the twentieth floor. But we don't know which. We'll take one that goes to every floor, and I'll try to track him as we ascend." She didn't want to try explaining how to her helper.

They had to wait a long time, but since most of the people went for the other cars, when they finally stepped into one they had some privacy, all its passengers having rapidly exited into the lobby. It was probably time to inform Nye about Professor John, before someone got on at another floor.

Anya pushed the button for the top floor. She glanced over at Nye, who watched the doors close in front of them with a broad smile, and tried to think how to broach the subject of the professor's death.

Nye looked down at her watch and then turned to Anya. "Why is my watch not showing anything— besides the blip for you in the center of the screen?"

Anya sighed. "It's programmed to help you find your leader, and you've found me. Now it's become useless. Mine is for finding my helpers, which I'm still trying to do." *But once I've found Turner, will it help me find the others?*

Anya held her device up so she could keep one eye on the screen and one on the changing numbers displayed above the doors. She might not have the time to break the news gently, so she'd better get it over with. "The professor's dead."

"What?" Anya could feel Nye's stare on the side of her face as the woman asked again, "What do you mean?"

"He was killed just as we came through. An accident." Anya couldn't close her eyes to the tears, so she just clenched her jaw and stared straight ahead. "Everything has been one big accident."

"Then what do we do now? We can't cancel the research project." The pitch of Nye's voice was ascending. "We can't just regroup and go home."

Anya shook her head. "We couldn't if we wanted to. The professor's device was destroyed."

She'd noticed earlier a video camera up in the corner of the elevator, and now she pointed it out to Nye. Anya held a finger to her lips to put an end to the conversation. She'd no idea if the thing picked up sound, but this prevented Nye from asking further questions.

The woman knew the worst of it now. More discussion could wait, and maybe later Anya would be better able to talk about it.

The silence was hard, too, but it wasn't long before the blip appeared on the locator screen. Anya quickly noted the current floor. *Twelve.* Since there was no thirteenth floor, that would put Turner on the thirty-third, or thereabouts. She hit the appropriate button.

They continued without a single word between them. Nye's expression was blank, and Anya had no idea if the girl was mad, sad, or simply following the stricture for silence. She did start fidgeting after a while. The elevator stopped occasionally and a few people got on to share the ride, but finally it landed them on the thirty-third floor.

The elevator doors opened to reveal a plush carpeted lobby with a wide arc of marble-topped desk and a receptionist behind it. Anya stepped out with trepidation, her mute helper beside her.

"Excuse us. We're looking for a friend of ours who may be lost. A young man—a handsome young man."

The bored receptionist perked up at the last bit. "How good looking? Like a star?"

A star? "I don't think anyone could be that brilliant, but Nye here is pretty bright."

The woman gave Anya a funny look and started laughing. Since people didn't generally find Anya to be amusing, she suspected she'd made some kind of mistake. It augured well that it had been taken for a joke. She imagined they'd all be erring all over the place and hoped they'd continue to be found just as amusing by the natives.

She glanced over at Nye. "I don't think he could have been on this floor. Turner's not a man women can fail to notice."

The receptionist's eyes darted to both Anya and Nye's ring fingers, which was heartening. It seemed that even in this time period, women knew to check whether another might have a prior claim. So far no one had a claim on Turner.

The woman smiled at them. "I did hear of some kind of commotion on thirty-four. But I'm not allowed to leave my desk without a replacement." She looked hopefully at Anya and Nye. "I could take one of you there—if the other stayed here."

Anya shook her head. "I'm sorry." It would be an unnecessary delay, and just so this woman could engage in a hunt Anya knew to be useless.

She led Nye back to the elevators. They waited in silence with their backs to the lobby, both aware of the glare they were getting. It felt like forever.

Finally a car came that was going up, and it took them to the floor above. There they emerged into a far more utilitarian lobby, and one whose attendant was absent. Anya nodded to herself. No rules about not leaving one's post would apply to a woman who had actually *met* Turner.

With Nye following behind, Anya stepped past the desk and pushed through two large glass doors into a busy office suite. She paused and checked the picture she'd taken with her watch. The whole floor was occupied by American Widgets, Inc.—though the directory didn't specify the nature of their business. When she looked up again, Nye was gone.

Anya wished she had a nose for coffee, sure that would lead her straight to her errant helper, but she had another wayward assistant to find. She closed her eyes and used her ears—and after a few minutes of filtering out the different background noises, she identified the proper one. Then she headed in the direction of the giggling.

Thankfully all the male workers were busy with their own tasks and disregarded Anya's presence. The same didn't hold true for the crowd of women in skirt suits gathered in the break room, who definitely noticed her entrance. Anya didn't mind—she had found both her helpers.

Nye was in a corner being ignored as she communed with a cup of coffee. Turner was pressed up against a counter by the ladies cooing over him, and looking uncomfortable with a sheepish grin. Knowing she did not belong here, Anya didn't wait to be challenged by the hostile crowd.

"Turner!"

The poor man with his thick blond mane and perfect complexion stood and looked over the women pressing around him and right into her eyes and blushed. She glared, thankful that she was immune to the effect he had—one of the reasons, she imagined, he'd been assigned to her team. She couldn't guess why Nye was her problem, but John was no longer available to ask. *The professor.* It would be easier if she thought of him like that.

She held Turner's gaze. "Grab Nye and her coffee and get a move on."

She turned on her heel and marched off before the ladies got started with the complaints, confident Turner would follow instructions. She stalked back through the offices and lobby to push those elevator buttons. She'd rather not have to stick around here very long.

A minute later Turner arrived with Nye in tow. At least the girl had gotten her coffee. Anya looked around the still empty lobby, then turned to Nye.

"Tell Turner what's been happening before the elevator gets here." *So I won't have to go through it again.*

She listened to Nye's short, confused summary and realized how little she'd told the girl, but then Anya didn't know much more herself. They were all winging it. And they'd have to keep making it up as they went along, because the professor had made no plans for dealing with this kind of catastrophe.

The three of them filed quickly into the elevator when it came. Nye put a finger to her lips to silence Turner, then pointed at the camera above. Anya casually checked her watch and was relieved to see an indication of what direction would lead them to find the next of their number. *North.*

She had no idea which member of what team it pointed to, or what kind of trouble he or she might be in. But she'd found both her own helpers and it felt good. Once Anya brought all the Travelers together, then they could face the difficult truth and try solving the serious problems.

Though she'd better focus first on gathering her flock, which could be a big enough challenge.

Chapter 2

A Desperate Embrace

June 30th, 2000 East Harlem

MATT danced down the sidewalk to the strings of Mozart's Quartet in C Major. The notes flowed from his headphones as he waved his hands in the air like a crazed conductor, fully aware of how he looked. It was a form of protective camouflage. Most pedestrians avoided him without seeming to, which suited him just fine.

Even though his ears were absorbed in the music, the rest of his senses were finely attuned to his environment, belying the illusion of obliviousness. His arms might be flailing, but his skin stayed sensitive to the vibrations of movement around him. His eyes darted around as he scanned for signs of trouble. As always, he hoped to make it to class without incident—which was why he noticed what was coming toward him in the distance.

The first image that flashed into his head was the redhead who walked slow and looked disoriented and carried an expensive bag. She couldn't have made herself any more of a target if she'd tried.

Then his eyes jumped to the three delinquents strolling behind her and trying to look casual. Their intentions were obvious. The third thing Matt saw was that he was too far away to stop what was about to happen.

These three pictures leapt into his mind at the same time, alarm bells going off in his cerebral cortex as his frontal lobe snapped him into action. He darted forward, headphones flying off behind him. He ran even as he realized the futility in the back of his brain—the hoodlums had already crowded behind the woman as he was crying out. One grabbed her purse while the other two pushed her down. He let them run right past him. His attention was on the redhead, and she needed his help.

She had toppled on her heels when pushed, collapsing into the iron gate that led to the basement entrance of a nearby building. He'd seen her hit her head on the metal bars, and she wasn't getting up.

Matt raced to her crumpled form while people walked past ignoring them both as they'd ignored her attackers. He thought it might be dangerous to move her, so he tried to be careful as he checked out her injuries, wishing he had more knowledge of first aid. Her scalp was bleeding badly, but he saw nothing more serious than that gruesome scrape.

She moaned and tried to sit up. "My bag."

"Don't move." Matt attempted to hold her still, but she kept shifting around.

"My purse?" Her voice sounded a bit stronger, and she turned to look up at him.

"I'm sorry," he told her. "They got your bag."

"But I need it."

Matt shook his head. "It's long gone. Hopefully you can replace whatever was in it."

Her eyes focused on his, and he saw they were a brilliant, crystal blue. "There wasn't anything *in* it. But it was a genuine reproduction antique."

Matt held his finger in front of her and moved it from side to side. That was how they did it on television. Her eyes moved back and forth following his finger with a puzzled expression. She might have a concussion, but he couldn't tell.

She glared at him. "Get my bag back."

Matt shook his head and tried to remember the other things doctors on TV did. "Do you know your name?"

"Page." The redhead frowned up at him. "What about my purse?"

23

"Forget that." He was growing more concerned about her mental state. "Can you tell me your last name?"

She just gave him a long, blank look.

Matt frowned at her. "Do you know who's President?"

"Maybe. It depends. Have you had the election yet? Is Florida still counting?" Page stared at him. "And could you also tell me what *your* name is, and how I'm going to get my bag back?"

"Matt. Matt Walker. And it would be easier to buy a new purse."

She looked straight into his eyes, and he could see the wheels turning behind *her* eyes. And whatever she was thinking about, it wasn't him. She definitely needed help, but he couldn't take the chance of calling for an ambulance—it would take them far too long to show up in this neighborhood, and when they did, they'd probably take her in for a psychiatric evaluation, and he didn't want that. Thankfully, he had another option.

Page started to sit up again, and despite the risk he helped her. If he was going to get her to the clinic, she'd need to be able to walk on her own or with a little assistance from him.

"Can you stand up? Is anything broken?" Matt worried he might be making things worse. "Do you think you can walk? If not, stay here, and I'll go get help." Though he didn't care much for that idea in this area.

Page reached out to grab his arm. "Don't leave. Not until the others find me."

"Others?" Matt looked around, but no one was paying them any attention. "Look, I've got a friend who can get you checked out." He was glad his good friend *was* a doctor. "He's a resident, but he's close enough to being a real doctor—and he volunteers at a clinic near here. They can fix you up. Alright?"

Page nodded vaguely, and he wrapped his arm around her back and slowly helped her to her feet.

She glanced sideways at him. "I think I bruised something. Matt."

No doubt. "You think you can manage a couple blocks? You can lean on me."

Page nodded, more definite than before. "But I can't waste too much time. My helpers will be looking for me."

Matt grinned. He wondered if those helpers of hers wore white coats. "For now, I'll be your helper. You can worry about contacting somebody to come and get you after you've been helped yourself."

He looked down and saw her heels were unbroken and hoped that held true for Page herself. He made sure to bear most of her weight as she hobbled along with him down the sidewalk and around the next corner.

To Matt it seemed to take them forever to travel the two and a half blocks to the Empire City Clinic. It would be best if his friend were on duty, but regardless, the staff there knew him, and he believed Page would get good care whatever her situation.

As he half carried her, he tried to figure out as much about this redhead as he could. She wasn't a New Yorker. She definitely acted like a tourist—a visitor who wore heels she couldn't properly walk in and carried an expensive but empty bag and wore a man's wristwatch. Matt wondered if she even had any identification on her.

What she was, was a puzzle.

A nurse rushed out of the lobby when they finally reached the sliding glass doors of the clinic, and she helped him carry Page inside.

Matt grinned. "Morning, Marcia."

Her lips were pressed tight as she took Page's other side and looked at him. "You're such a klutz, Walker. At least this time you brought your victim in yourself. This time you'll pay the bill, too."

Matt chuckled. If he hadn't known Marcia, he wouldn't have known this was her idea of humor.

"She says her name is Page. But she's not processing very well—maybe a concussion?"

Marcia gently settled Page into an empty wheelchair sitting in the lobby. "You let us decide what she might be suffering from—other than you."

Matt followed her in as she wheeled Page back to the urgent care section.

Marcia glanced over her shoulder at him. "You don't need to come along. We'll take proper care of your Page."

"Oh, no. I'm sticking with this one until I find out her story."

"You don't know how she was injured?"

"I saw that. Purse snatchers. I mean I want to know who she is. I don't even know if she has any identification, or anything to say who to contact."

"We'll worry about that." Marcia smirked. "Did you trying asking her?"

She leaned down to look Page in the face. "You want us to get a hold of somebody for you, sweetie? Tell them you're here?"

Page looked back at the nurse. "I need Tate and Bailey. But they know how to find me."

Marcia frowned and looked back at Matt. "I see what you mean."

She wheeled Page over to a station with various medical equipment and sat down on a metal stool. She clamped things on Page's fingers to monitor her heart rate and oxygenation, and started wrapping a blood pressure cuff around Page's upper arm.

Matt hovered. "Well? How is she?"

"Be quiet." Marcia pumped away and focused on taking Page's blood pressure and noting everything down on a chart. "You need a sense of humor like Doctor Wallace."

"If my parents had given me a name like Harding, I'd have had no choice but to develop a sense of humor. He's not around?"

"It's still morning, isn't it? What do you think?" Marcia almost smiled. Then she shone a pen light in Page's pupils. "If she's got a concussion it must be pretty mild. I'll patch her up and see if she's got any ID. Now you—get out of here."

Marcia pushed him away and drew the curtain closed around them. She wouldn't need Matt's help to take care of Page, but he wouldn't go far until he knew what, if anything, the nurse had managed to discover about this mystery girl.

He sauntered out to one of the waiting rooms and got himself a cup of terrifyingly bad coffee from the vending machine. He eased himself into one of the hard plastic chairs, stretching out his legs.

This business would make him late for the seminar on black hole mechanics, but the mysteries of the universe were familiar to him. The riddle of the redhead was new.

Matt had closed his eyes and let his mind wander when Marcia came up and slapped him on the shoulder. She must have thought he'd fallen asleep with the coffee in his hand. "I've got your girlfriend settled now, if you want to come and see her."

Matt stood up and stretched his arms, tossing the full cup into the nearby trash can. "Did you find out her last name?"

"No." Marcia frowned. "She doesn't have any identification, and she says she doesn't have a 'last name'—just the one. She's a comedienne."

"Did she have anything on her that might give a clue as to who she is or where she belongs?"

"Pretty fancy clothes, but no labels. And that man's watch." Marcia gave him a sly look. "Which belongs to her *actual* boyfriend if you ask me. Her stolen purse would've had all her ID, and anything else that might've been useful."

Matt frowned. "She said there was nothing in her purse."

Marcia gave him one of those looks women often gave him, the kind that said men know nothing. "Whatever she said to you, she's not saying much of anything to me. Perhaps you can get her to tell you more—something that might help us get a line on who to contact. Or we *will* stick you with the bill."

"As if I needed any extra motivation to find out who she is."

Marcia led him to where Page was half-reclined in a hospital bed in a room with five other beds. The curtains were drawn around the rest, so he had no idea who they might be sharing the room with. Not that there was any privacy here to begin with.

Page lay there with a big white bandage on the side of her head, staring into the distance. She did not seem to be aware of their presence. Yet. Matt found her straight red hair falling just to her shoulders quite fetching. <u>He even thought her attractive in that hospital gown</u>—there was no need for the fancy clothes.

He shook himself. Definitely out of his league, and the man's watch probably *did* mean she had a boyfriend. He couldn't help but notice though, that she wore no ring.

Marcia frowned down at her patient. "No real symptoms of concussion, but I'm worried about her nonetheless. Try to keep her from falling asleep, at least for a couple hours if you can." She glanced at Matt. "Try talking to her. She's your responsibility, so stick around until we know more. I'll be around fairly often to check on her condition."

The nurse left, presumably to check up on other patients. As she departed, Page turned to Matt with a clear gaze. "Your friend is awfully nosy."

"She has a duty. A legal one, in addition to her moral obligation. To contact someone who can take care of you." *And pay the bill.*

"She said I'm *your* responsibility. Isn't that sufficient?" Page squinted at him for a long moment. "She also said I could trust you—that you're 'honest as your legs are long.'"

Matt smiled. "They only look long to you short people. And I wouldn't trust me if I were you." He looked at the neat bandage messing her hair up and grinned. "She got you cleaned up proper, anyway. How are you feeling now?"

"Sore. And she took my clothes and gave them to someone else."

Matt shook his head. "I imagine they'll be folded away in one of those drawers." He nodded at the chest beside her. On top of it sat that watch of hers. "When you're ready to leave, they'll want you wearing your own clothes. Which would probably be a good idea, since the gown your wearing now doesn't belong to you."

Page pinched at the paper garment. "Gown? I might as well be wearing my thesis."

Matt's ears perked up. "Your thesis? What's it about?" He figured she was a mathematician. Math geeks were vague and hard to understand.

"Statistical models of twentieth century dating rituals."

Matt blinked. Math geeks were bad enough— social statisticians were beyond his comprehension. "I'm a graduate student at GTI. Theoretical Physics. I don't suppose you go to Goth Tech?"

She shook her head. "You're a nerd, then?"

Matt blinked again. "Yes, I suppose I am." *Just call me Mr. Kettle.*

Page nodded to herself. "I'm looking for a ball-room dancer."

Matt was glad he'd tossed his coffee or he might have spilled it all over himself. *Does that mean she doesn't already have a boyfriend, or that he's not a dancer?*

"That might be a challenge." He shook his head again. "I'm looking for someone who'll know what to do with you. Family or friends?"

"My helpers, Tate and Bailey. They'll find me. They won't have much choice, since they'll be stuck without me."

"That *would* be tragic." Which sounded sarcastic. "A tragedy to be without you, I mean." And that sounded like a sappy pick-up line. "Why don't you give them a call?"

Page shook her head. "How? The communication technologies you use are always changing. We couldn't prepare."

Matt realized he was scratching the top of his head as he wondered if this redhead was some kind of alien. *A beautiful math geek from outer space.* It sounded like a bad movie.

Marcia kept accusing him of not having a sense of humor, but he found the whole world amusing—it was all one big, bizarre comedy routine. He just laughed on the inside so hard it hurt. Page not only bemused him, she thoroughly perplexed him.

Matt spoke slowly. "If you can't call them, and they can't call you—" Matt waited for Page's nod. "How in the world do you expect them to be able to find you?" He thought about her bizarre behavior. "You're not all 'psychics'—are you?"

Page gave him a long, level look. "You do have GPS, don't you?"

"Global Positioning Satellites. Of course." He glanced over at the watch. It had to have some sort of GPS tracking, and that reeked of espionage. But he had a hard time seeing Page as a spy. *Government research?* She didn't seem the sort of scientist he'd expect to find doing highly classified work. He *was* having trouble figuring her out.

She must have seen his look. "Hand it to me."

Matt hesitated. "Is there any particular reason you wear a man's watch?" Marcia had asked him to try some questions, so it wasn't like he was prying.

Page looked at him blankly. "*Man's* watch?"

Matt sighed. That might mean she didn't have a boyfriend, or it might be her general vagueness. He was beginning to suspect this might be her normal state and not a result of hitting her head.

He stretched over and grabbed the watch. *GPS?* It was hard black plastic—not the classy kind of gift a rich boyfriend might've given her. But it had to be pretty expensive if it had satellite tracking and who knew what other advanced functions.

Matt wondered if she'd bought it for some practical application. "You're lucky they didn't take this too, if it's the only way your friends can locate you." He hadn't thought of Page as being practical. "What else can this thing do?"

She stretched out her hand. "Give it to me, and I'll show you."

He hesitated again. This watch was starting to intrigue him almost as much as the woman herself. He held it up in front of his face to take a closer look at the screen. Time and date. Latitude and longitude. He'd likely have to press some buttons to get to the other functions.

"Are you hard of hearing?" Page glared at him. "It's my watch, and I'd appreciate it if you'd hand it over. Right now."

He didn't want to upset her, yet he kept hold of the watch. He was supposed to be finding out about her, which he wanted to do anyway—and he didn't want to hang around and see if her friends would be more forthcoming than she'd been. He turned the watch over to examine its back.

There was no brand name or maker's mark— only a designation that seemed too short for a serial number. *LD—2.* He turned it over again and made sure he hadn't missed a manufacturer there. It had to be a prototype. He started to put the watch in her waiting palm, but his curiosity stopped him.

Matt glanced from the watch to Page. "Is this experimental? Some kind of government project?" He was beginning to buy into that notion now. "Am I cleared to learn about its secret abilities?" Which was sarcastic again.

"It *is* research, but not in the way *you* mean it. Please give it to me."

For some reason he still felt reluctant to hand it over, felt some connection to this watch. Or to Page through the watch? And holding on to it for another minute wouldn't hurt, should be all he needed to see what was so special about it. "I'm pretty smart. I bet I can figure out how to work this thing."

He pushed a couple different buttons and found one that cycled through a series of screens that all seemed simple enough—but he was having a hard time understanding exactly what they were for. He noticed Page was growing increasingly agitated, but a few more seconds should satisfy his curiosity.

She let her empty hand fall to the bed. "Please. Matt. You don't understand."

"Don't be distressed. I'll be careful not to break anything." And he began to try pushing those other buttons while he was on various screens to see what happened.

Page's voice was shrill with alarm as she yelped, "Stop messing about, Matt." And she stretched out her hand again, pleading.

Matt's heart ached to hear her like that. Relenting, he began to give the watch back—and out of the corner of his eye saw Marcia appearing at the door. If she had heard the panic in Page's voice, the nurse would have some harsh words for him.

And he didn't want her to misunderstand. Trying to think how he could explain, he automatically tightened his grip on the watch. Just as Page threw herself forward and wrapped her arms around him. And in that moment, everything except the redhead clinging to him ceased to exist.

Chapter 3

And Then There were Eight

June 30th, 2000 The Upper West Side

SAMANTHA crouched down carefully to massage her swiftly swelling ankle. The flow of pedestrians parted around her like a river diverting around an island—and she felt like that island, alone and isolated and gradually being worn down by the water. She blamed her own slow reflexes.

When she'd arrived on the edge of a wide stone step, she'd stiffened as her left foot simply dropped straight down all the way to the lower step. She had felt the joint twist and the ankle sprain. She'd wanted to sit down right there and have a good cry, but looking around and not seeing any of the others had shocked her out of the temptation.

Sam had kept her weight on the good foot and immediately checked her watch. She'd landed right in the center of New York City and the middle of the year two thousand. As she was supposed to. *Where then is everyone else?*

She'd switched to the locator screen to see the red bar showing her leader Harold to the south but out of range. She hadn't wasted any time trying to understand why they had become separated. Keeping her weight off her left ankle as much as possible, she'd hobbled down the wide stairs to the sidewalk and then down the next street in the direction indicated.

She'd only even glanced at the Rose Window at the Cathedral of St. John the Divine. She'd return and bask later, after she'd found the others. She'd come on her own if she had to, since the rest with their different interests and specialties might not be so inclined. Then she could have a good long look around. But not now, not yet.

Kneeling on the sidewalk three blocks south of where she'd arrived, she continued massaging her ankle with one hand while checking her watch. Now Harold was somewhere to the southwest. Either he had moved or she was getting close, but whichever it was, she didn't want to dally. So she straightened with reluctance and limped as fast as she could the rest of the block to the next intersection.

Sam had to hurry to cross with the light over to the other side of the busy street, all the while being jostled by the other pedestrians and clenching her teeth against the pain. When she reached the opposite corner, she saw the blip appear on her locator screen. Harold, at last.

Maybe her leader would like to take a nice long rest somewhere. He did enjoy taking his ease—she normally found that frustrating, but today would be different. She would appreciate Harold.

Sam slowed her pace as she kept her eye on the watch face. Halfway down the block she turned and swept her eyes across the far sidewalk, looking for her leader. She saw his bald pate first, as he stood against the brick wall in the mouth of the narrow alleyway between two buildings.

Then she noticed Kirin with her long, beautiful black hair, pressing Harold against that wall as she moved in for a kiss. *Not the time or the place, Harold.* Sam shook her head. Kirin had been working on Harold before they'd left, and Sam despaired of the woman ever changing her ways. Harold should have known better.

Sam stood staring at the pair and giving her ankle a rest. Despite the pain, she wanted to rush over and reunite with her team—but she didn't want to embarrass her leader by interrupting his moment of weakness. Neither of them would thank her.

She found herself fascinated. She'd never been able to bring herself to chase after a man, no matter how attracted, and watching Kirin pressing herself against Harold was like looking through a window into another world.

Even from the opposite side of the street, Sam could see them kissing. Locked together in a long embrace, Harold held Kirin with more strength and passion than Sam would have thought possible. But then his grip loosened and Kirin backed away from her prey. Sam was too far to see the expressions on their faces, but she bet they were both smiling. She could imagine the peculiar curl of Kirin's lips in her mind's eye.

Then Harold slid down the brick wall—just sat there on the ground and stayed that way, still, with his head lying back against the bricks. Kirin stood there for a moment looking down at him before she finally knelt to help the man.

She reached out to grab his hand. Then after a minute she stood up again, raising herself to her full height augmented by those spiky heels.

The woman turned and looked straight at Sam. There was a flash of inexplicable electricity between the two women, then Kirin turned and walked fast down the alley toward the other end, leaving Harold right where he sat. Sam felt like she was frozen in that particular moment in time.

Something was wrong. Sam felt it in her heart, and her feet must have felt it too, because she was stumbling out into the street before she knew what she was doing. She made as straight a line for Harold as she could, dodging honking cars and fighting not to fall flat on her face.

She rolled over the hood of a cab that stopped right in front of her. With her ankle already injured she supposed it didn't make much difference if she bruised the rest of her body—as long as she didn't demand too much of that ankle.

At least she managed to get to the other side of the street without killing herself. She limped to the mouth of the alley and leaned over to look Harold in the eye—there remained some life in him but it was fading fast. He tried to say something to her, but all that came out of his mouth was a bubble of blood.

That was when Sam looked down and saw the neat little wound. So little blood around such a tiny hole in his shirt, right through the ribs underneath his heart. She glanced around to see the slim stiletto lying on the ground just a few feet away.

Sam turned back to speak to her leader. Harold wasn't there anymore though, just his lifeless shell with its hand across his belly as if he'd tried to reach for her. She wanted to cry. She felt the tears welling up, and as she tried to blink them away she noticed that Harold's watch was gone. *Of course.*

The tears dried. Poor Harold had been led into this trap, and she felt sorry for him. More than that though, Sam felt a blinding anger toward Kirin, a furnace blazing in her heart. The woman had just tossed the murder weapon on the ground with her fingerprints all over it—no doubt because she had known it didn't matter. Kirin already had the perfect plan for escaping justice.

Well, Sam wouldn't let that happen. She could think about the rest of it later—right now, Kirin was putting more distance between them, and Sam had to prevent that, no matter what it might do to her injured ankle. That meant she had to run.

She stepped away from the corpse, turned, and sprinted for the other end of the alley. She had to grind down so hard against the pain she felt it would crack her teeth as she pounded across the pavement and leapt over the detritus in her way. But she'd no choice if she wanted to catch her quarry.

Unaware of Sam's injury, Kirin would assume she was being pursued full speed and make haste herself in an effort to lose Sam. And all Kirin needed to do was get far enough away to Travel without her pursuer being in range to be caught in the field. If she managed that, Sam would lose any hope of finding her.

Sam didn't dare glance at her locator to check, but Kirin might already be that far away—she could only hope Kirin was too preoccupied with running away to notice if that had occurred. A slim thread of hope indeed.

At the south end of the alley, Sam checked her watch and quickly lifted her head to the left to scan the crowd and pick out her target. Kirin had already crossed to the next block to the east and was moving fast. One advantage Sam had was the other woman's height and long, flowing jet-black hair—Sam should be able to keep Kirin in sight without constantly checking her watch.

Sam did follow that distinctive head as she hurried through the crowd of pedestrians. And as she felt another stab of sharp pain up her leg, she reminded herself that she had another advantage—Kirin's tight skirt and high heels would restrict her movement.

It was sweltering, and Sam was glad she'd worn shorts for the anticipated summer weather because it also meant she moved free. And with her running shoes on, hopefully it would be enough to compensate for the sprain.

Kirin didn't turn back to look for her pursuer, but she could check her locator. Though if she did, Sam never saw. She was glad for once that her own lack of height might help obscure her from view. If only the fool woman would waste the time trying to look back.

Kirin must've taken Harold's leader device because it could Travel on its own—neither Sam's nor Kirin's helper watches had that ability. They only worked in proximity to a device like Harold's. With that now in her possession, Kirin could Travel when she pleased, and if Sam were out of the range of the field, she wouldn't be able to follow the murderess through time.

And Kirin had only to Travel into the past to get beyond the reach of whatever authorities might be seeking justice for Harold.

Sam knew she had been given the responsibility for stopping Kirin. The woman had murdered Harold, and Sam was a witness, the only witness to the evil act, the only one who *knew.* More than that she understood the further crimes Kirin could commit with Harold's device and the access it gave to Travel throughout history. Clearly the woman was without the conscience which would prevent her from doing terrible things. Sam was the only person who was in a position to stop that.

So she kept running, trying to ignore the pain and the fear, to avoid thinking about the extra damage she was doing to her ankle. But she failed.

Sam felt the tears welling up again even as she ran. Not for Harold this time, or even for the pain, though she could blame that if she wanted. No, she cried because she was destroying herself.

Sam had always been able to run like the wind, ever since she was a little girl, and it made her feel alive and free. Now she was likely doing permanent and irreparable injury to her ankle. She might not run again. She'd be fortunate if she could still walk properly after this, and she couldn't imagine being that person. It wouldn't be her.

She turned her tears into flight, increasing her speed as she stoked the fire of anger burning in her belly. Even so she could tell she was losing ground to Kirin. The woman would be checking her watch, so Sam didn't have to worry about slowing down to check her own in order to know whether or not she was still in range. She focused on her quarry.

She also needed to pay attention to the people and objects in her path. People tended to get out of Kirin's way, but they ignored small Samantha and forced her to weave around them. That slowed her down almost as much as her ankle.

Sam ran down one painfully long block, then a short one, and by the time she had crossed the next intersection, the distance between herself and Kirin had lengthened considerably.

Sam estimated that she might've already fallen out of range. She tried to pour on more speed, but her ankle refused to comply—it wasn't just the pain she was fighting, her foot wasn't working right. She found herself slowing down.

She struggled forward, but all the willpower she could pour into her legs failed to transfer into faster movement. Soon she would likely catapult herself into the pavement.

With the tears flowing freely now, Sam looked into the distance where she saw Kirin crossing over to the entrance into a massive park in the middle of the city. The woman almost danced up some stairs, even wearing those heels, and it almost made Sam *want* to cry. She had failed.

Kirin turned at the top of those stairs and gazed behind her, searching. Sam was too far away to see the woman's eyes, but she felt them connect, and it seemed they were staring right into each other. She knew when the other woman glanced down at her locator. Sam didn't need to check her own to know she was well outside the range of the Travel field.

She could sense Kirin's smile of triumph as the woman fiddled with the watch, Harold's device, so she could Travel—away from Sam and away from justice.

Sam stopped fighting the tears then, and her eyes flooded. The whole world blurred through the water. And then it vanished.

Chapter 4

The Former Farmer's Tale

June 30th, 2000 Midtown Manhattan

ANYA felt like a mother duck leading her children across the street. Turner would be the more mature since he followed her lead as she took them into the park. Nye came straggling after.

Now that the girl had her coffee she'd returned to mooning after her colleague. She didn't seem to be obsessed—she appeared to enjoy ogling the man as a pastime. If it kept her from straying from their little flock, so much the better.

Both of Anya's helpers had begun a barrage of questions as soon as they'd left the oppressive office building and returned to the open, if unhealthy, air. She had cut them short. Discussion of their myriad problems could wait until they had found the other Travelers, then they could *all* talk it over.

Of course Turner went quiet. Nye clearly wanted to continue pestering Anya about what they were going to do, but the girl was too busy trying to drink her coffee and keep up with Turner's long strides at the same time to press the issue.

Anya herself focused on following the directions indicated by her locator because she wanted to find the other teams as soon as possible. It also kept her from thinking too much about what had happened to John. *An added benefit.* And gathering the rest of her brood *was* paramount.

Anya had hustled down block after block along the busy morning sidewalks with only the barest of glances for potential hazards. She had no attention to spare on seeing the sights. When her watch led to this giant park in the middle of the city though, she decided to enjoy it.

So she entered the park with her ducklings trailing, then began gazing back and forth between the lush surroundings and her locator screen. She was startled when she glanced down and saw the red bar had been replaced by a white blip. She lifted up her head and looked into the distance and saw a fellow Traveler—who had raised his own head in a similar fashion and was staring at her. *Wait. Was there no more red bar?*

She was distracted by Nye piping up from behind. "I know there were references to this 'Central Park' but I never expected it would be so big. By the time—"

Anya glanced back over her shoulder. "Yes, I'm sure we'll discover a lot of what we thought we knew was wrong. But please save the discourse for later. We've found Tate." *Or he's found us.*

She turned back to try to see her friend's face as she strode toward him down the cement walkway. *Dear Tate.* Her tears wanted to well up again, this time in joy. She had lost John, but this farmer also held a special place in her heart.

Like her, he'd given up his life and his former career in order to work on this project—despite the fact they were both too old for all this gallivanting around. She dashed ahead to speed their reunion, trusting Turner and Nye would catch up.

Tate kept walking at the same steady pace, continuing to check his watch even though he could see her rushing at him. *Good old Tate.* His sunburned face smiled at her when he *was* looking up.

"Tate!" His broad, weathered face was surely a sight for sore eyes. Anya reached him and grabbed his large, calloused hands with relief.

Tate took her hands in his. "Professor Anya."

She frowned. "Call me 'Leader'. John was the only true professor." His death was too raw and her title too new. She hadn't felt as if she'd earned the upgrade and doubted she ever would.

"Was?" Tate's smile slowly faded.

Anya's own face fell. "When we came through, the professor landed in the middle of the street. He never even had the time to realize—"

"Then consider that a blessing."

"Yes. Thank you." Trust Tate to see right to the heart of things. People tended to think he was slow, and he was in a way, but he tended to know right off the important things. "And his device was smashed in the accident. I haven't had time to look closely, but I suspect it's beyond any hope of repair."

Tate's smile returned. "Well, I trust you'll work something out."

His eyes drifted over her shoulder and she assumed her helpers had caught up. "Before we worry about solving any of the other problems we need to hurry up and find the rest."

Anya checked her locator screen and frowned at what she saw. She could feel the other three staring at her. Her brain must have frozen over for her to just stand there like a statue.

Nye was the first to pipe up. "What is it?" She'd finished her coffee now, and Anya wouldn't be able to keep her quiet or put off answering questions.

"I'm not sure." Anya hesitated to speculate out loud. She lifted her head and took a good long look around. She spotted an empty table and benches in the distance and nodded in that direction. "Let's sit down and relax while we talk."

Tate followed her gesture. "I would appreciate giving these feet a rest."

He and Anya walked to the table with Nye and Turner following. When all four had sat, the three helpers turned their waiting eyes on Anya, but she didn't want to jump to conclusions. Their watches would be no help while she was anywhere near, so she scrutinized her own for a long, drawn out moment, thinking.

"My locator app isn't showing anything." Anya corrected herself immediately. "I mean, you three are all showing up as blips right in the center. But a red bar should be blinking to show the direction of the nearest Traveler outside the range of the field. But there's nothing."

Nye looked clueless and confused. Turner was thoughtful. Tate frowned at the ground and cleared his throat before he lifted his eyes to meet Anya's.

"I think maybe you should hear my story." Tate shook his head. "I don't understand it myself, but it might explain some things."

Anya gave him an encouraging smile.

Tate glanced at the other two to include them in his tale. "When I arrived and couldn't see any of the rest of my team, I started searching for Page."

Anya nodded. Tate would've been most conscientious about tracking down his leader. "Bailey and Page should've arrived close to you. Closer than the rest of us anyway." She cast a narrow glance at *her* two helpers. "Using your device to home in on your team leader right away. Exactly what you should've done. Quite proper." She looked back to Tate. "But couldn't you find Page?"

"No." Tate frowned. "I got a direction on her. At least that's what I assumed. And I was following the trail."

Anya assumed he'd followed it at a slow, steady pace. "Go on."

"Well, I was keeping a close eye on the screen and then all of a sudden the direction changed."

"Yes, when you get close then—"

But Tate was shaking his head. "It went from north to west. I stood and stared at it for a while, and then it went back to pointing north."

"Perhaps if another leader, and I mean Harold since it wasn't me, happened to be close enough—" Anya paused. "And if Page were moving away from you, that might account for it." She shrugged. "The locator apps on your helper devices were meant to lock onto whatever leader device is in closest physical proximity. So it might've switched between the two of them if the conditions were right. Was Harold anywhere around?"

Tate scratched his head. "I think I understand what you're saying. But if Harold was there I didn't see him."

"Even so, it's the only explanation I can think of that makes sense." Anya smiled. "I'm sorry. I need to let you get on with your story."

"No apology necessary, Leader." Tate frowned down at the surface of the table. "So I started heading north again, but it wasn't long before it switched to the south. I waited for a while, but when it stayed that way I turned around. I followed the directions and eventually my watch brought me into the park and straight to you."

Anya adjusted her long skirt on the bench and sat thinking things through again. They'd all gone through the orientation. Even if they'd paid attention though, none of them were as familiar with the devices as she was—how they were to be operated, and how they'd been programmed.

She made eye contact with each one of the helpers in turn. "I'll take this one piece at a time but I'll start with the only logical conclusion based on what we *do* know." She sighed and lifted her eyes to the sky. "Everyone but the four of us sitting here must have already Traveled away."

Nye piped up immediately. "What? How could they even do that so soon after we'd arrived. There's a twenty-four hour limit isn't there?"

Turner followed with his own question. "Leaving is what they were supposed to do, wasn't it?"

Anya shook her head. "We did plan to split up eventually, yes—that's why the leader devices even *have* a limited Travel capacity. But first the professor was going to help us get accustomed to this time period."

She laid her hands flat on the table and turned to Nye. "And twenty-four hours is the maximum amount of time it might take for a leader device to recharge before it can be used for Traveling, but we came through the field generated by the professor's. Only a minimal amount of power from our individual devices would have been depleted."

Tate frowned. "But Harold and Page both must have noticed how we were all separated on arrival. They should have waited." His face made it clear he couldn't understand why his leader had left without him. "Why didn't they wait?"

Anya sighed. "We can only speculate. But Page is flighty enough that she might have Traveled without making sure you were in range. I hope Bailey at least is with her, because she really needs a helper." Anya closed her eyes. "I'm surprised about Harold though, but he can be a pushover. Kirin or Sam or both might've prodded him into leaving early. And he must have taken them both along, since they're no longer here."

Nye was still energized. "Well, how do we find them then?"

"We don't. There's no way we can track them through time." *Not without the professor's device.* "And it would be foolish to try and chase them down blind. They'll have to find us." *And what are the odds of that?*

Tate was watching Anya think. "So what do we do now? Leader."

She gave them a weak smile. "We've got three challenges. The most important must be bringing the others back somehow. They won't know about the professor's death or the destruction of his device. So when he fails to show up and check on their progress, they'll have to realize *something* is wrong. And try to find out what. So, since we can't really go searching for them, maybe we can leave them some breadcrumbs to follow, to catch up to us where we'll be going."

Turner frowned. "Follow? Catch up? Where do we go? Wouldn't it be better to just stay where we are? Make it easier for them to find us?"

"Probably." Anya removed her hands from the table and folded them in her lap. "But how long do we wait? Because we have a couple other concerns. One is the research we came to do. The others are surely hard at work doing *their* research. The four of us could stay right here and do ours, but—"

Nye's hand shot into the air. "I vote for that."

Anya ignored her. "Our other problem, which I was getting to—if we can't get the professor's device working, how can we return home? I know we just left, and none of you are worried about that yet, but if we don't start thinking about it now..."

She felt the tears wanting to well up again and pushed them back down. The professor was home now, and she needed to focus on what she had to do. So she continued on. "My device can only Travel up to three years at once. It would take an awful long time for us to get home that way, and that's ignoring the problem of how we got separated when we came through. So we need a way to shoot three birds with one arrow."

Turner stood up and stretched his legs, gazing out across the park. "And how do we do that?"

"We'll have to Travel as a group, but that's too dangerous here in the city." *As we've found out the hard way.* "So we find someplace out in the country where we'll be able to find each other again easily if we get scattered. A home base."

Nye raised her hand to object. "But there's so much to learn studying this city."

Anya waved the girl down. "I'm not suggesting we leave it alone—just that we Travel to and from a more isolated location, a safer one. We can utilize the native transportation to return for research." If anyone other than Nye wished to come back to this city.

Nye lowered her hand. But it was Turner who'd been asking most of those questions.

Anya shifted off the bench and stood. "I think we should spend some time researching—it is what we came to do. But I propose that we make regular trips into the future. Say a year at a time. In that way, we'd at least be making our way slowly toward home at the same time."

Nye stood as well. "That would be good methodology for our research, too. We can document the changes over discrete periods of time."

Turner sucked air through his teeth. "I want to know what we're going to do about the others. The breadcrumbs?"

Anya nodded. "If we have a base of operations, if we're traveling in regular intervals we've decided on before hand, then we can find some way to leave messages for the rest. Telling them where and when they can find us."

Tate stood and smiled. "I guess you must have practiced with that metaphorical bow and arrow of yours, Leader, to shoot like that."

They were all on their feet now, looking to Anya. She was their leader, and she'd have to try her best to take care of them, and she imagined it would end up being quite a job. *But who else is there?*

Anya smoothed her dress and considered for a moment. "Our difficulties are only beginning. I'm just pointing out the only way I can see to start trying to address them all." She looked to make sure they were each paying close attention. "We'll have to figure out how to put this plan into action."

Tate nodded at her. "You don't have to manage all on your own, you know. We can help make it all work." He looked at Nye and Turner. "We wouldn't be here if we didn't each have something to contribute. So let's put our minds together."

Anya smiled at Tate. He'd be a *real* helper, and he was the only one of the three who wasn't hers—but she thought he understood what she was going through.

"Before we make any decisions, we need to eat. We'll think better on full stomachs. But before we can eat, we'll have to go to the bank and get access to our money. First things first, though."

Anya reached out and grabbed Nye's hand on her left and Tate took her right. "You're the former preacher, Turner, why don't you lead us in prayer?"

Chapter 5

Head over Heels

November 30th, 1998 Montauk Point

MATT all of a sudden stood on a cliff top, looking out across the Atlantic Ocean. Page no longer held him in a tight embrace, but her right arm was clasping his as her angry eyes burned into him. Then he felt the ground crumble from underneath her feet. She was falling and pulling him over the edge along with her.

He dropped straight down, flattening himself spread-eagle on the ground, stretching out over the eroding bluff. He held her arm with all his strength, her entire body dangling below. The harsh, bitterly cold wind whipped across his back, and the glare of the sun in his eyes forced him to squint.

Matt's arm was growing heavy with the effort of supporting her weight. "Stop flailing and see if you can get your feet up against the cliff face." Then he remembered that she was in bare feet. Or had been a few seconds ago when she'd been in the bed at the clinic. *What in creation had happened?*

Miraculously Page managed to get a foothold— the pull on his arm lessened. She hadn't screamed yet, but she did sound a little strained as she yelled up at him. "I could use some help here."

"Okay, I'm going to try and drag you up. Get ready."

He slowly rose up into a crouch so he could use his legs under him to brace and add some strength to his effort. He took a long, deep breath. Then he stood and yanked and leaned backward pushing as hard as he could with his heels, all in one motion.

Page came scrambling over the edge of the bluff and flew into Matt's arms. Again. He smiled, thinking he could get used to this kind of treatment. Page pushed him away and glared.

She glanced around then and yelped, "Where's my watch?"

Matt started to rub the top of his head. She was only now becoming hysterical when her life was no longer in danger. "The watch?"

Page looked back at the cliff. "The watch, you idiot. You were holding it when we Traveled. You should've still been holding it as we arrived." Her face was white. "You didn't drop it over the cliff, did you?"

Matt started to consider what had actually happened. *Teleportation?* He wouldn't have imagined seeing research that advanced in his lifetime, but he couldn't deny the evidence of his eyes. He looked around and knew where they were standing. And it was a far cry from where they'd been the moment before.

"My device!" Page dropped to her knees and started searching in the grass.

Matt tried to recall the details. The watch had been in his left hand when he dropped himself to the ground. His eyes zeroed in on the very spot, and he squatted to grab it before she could.

They both stood at the same time, and he then noticed the shape she was in—the paper gown she'd been wearing was torn and stained with dirt. Her knees were freshly scraped, as were her bare feet. And despite the big bandage on her head, the strong wind was blowing her red hair into a fury. And it only made her more beautiful. ♡ ℬ

Matt grinned. "You're quite a sight, you know."

She didn't forget to glare at Matt as she made a grab for the watch in his hand, but he snatched it away. She hugged herself against the cold wind as it whipped around them. "Give it to me."

Matt shook his head. "Not until you explain to me what's going on." He noticed she was shivering. "And that should wait until after we get you some warmer clothes." ✔(?)

Page clenched her teeth. "And how are you going to do that? I don't know where you've brought us—do you even have any idea what year you Traveled us to?"

What year? That implied *time* travel. He had a hard time believing that when she seemed so vague about everything.

Matt pointed down the coast to a lighthouse in the distance. "I do know *where* we are. Montauk Point. In Suffolk County." Matt saw the confusion on her face. "On Long Island."

"Long Island?" Page drew out the question as if she were tasting the words. "Isn't that somewhere near New York City?"

Matt shook his head. She looked and sounded like a mental case, but he was actually beginning to put stock in the idea that she was a time-traveler. It would be better than an extraterrestrial.

"That's kind of difficult to explain, to someone who doesn't already know." He looked back at the lighthouse. "Where we are right now, it's not technically part of New York City, but it's close enough. Most of the island *is* actually part of the city." Matt sighed. "Now let's get you some clothes."

Page scoffed. "And again, how do you propose to do that?"

Matt considered. It looked like early morning, and he couldn't see anyone in the immediate vicinity. Thankfully. *It must be the off season.* And then he realized it was far too cold for summer. If they really had time-traveled he had to believe that not only might it be a different year, but a different time of year. Somehow that was more difficult to accept. *Because it jars the senses.*

"I came out here once with a friend. I seem to remember there being a souvenir shop around here somewhere. It should have something better than what you're wearing now."

Page shivered again. "I don't have any money on me."

Matt pulled out his wallet and started counting. "I have some cash. It ought to be enough. If we've really traveled in time, I guess I shouldn't try to use my credit card."

"You need to check the dates on your money. If you've taken us into the past, you don't want to try and use money that was printed in the future."

The past? Matt scratched behind his ear. "And how will I know that, if I don't know the year." TB

Page bared her teeth in an approximation of a smile. "Indeed. Why should I say? You've yet to convince me that I can trust you."

Matt sighed. "Even so, we'll have to cooperate to a degree."

"Then consult that watch you're holding. *My* watch."

He glanced down warily, ready for another attempt to wrest the thing from him. What he saw on the watch face was the time and date. The thirtieth of November. Nineteen ninety-eight. They'd traveled into the past. *That'll set the cat among the pigeons.*

Page sighed. "Well? What year is it?"

Matt grinned. She looked enough like an escaped mental patient as it was. "I'm holding onto this until I get my own answers, remember?" *And so you don't run away on me.*

She cocked her head as she appraised him. "I think you know more than you should already. You aren't so stupid you haven't realized that we Traveled in time. To which idea you're adapting rather quickly."

Matt thought she sounded suspicious of him. "I *am* studying theoretical physics. So the theories of time travel *are* rather familiar to me." He smiled at her and reached out to grab her hand. "I don't want you running away from me before you've explained a bit more than that."

Page sniffed. "Even if you give me back my device, I can't Travel until it's recharged anyway."

Matt grinned. "And when I said I didn't want you skipping out on me, I wasn't just talking about time travel. Now, let's go get you some clothes."

He dragged Page inland until they reached the souvenir shop he remembered. He opened up his wallet to check that he had plenty of older bills that wouldn't raise any red flags. He certainly wouldn't dare try using his credit card.

He set her right in front of the shop window so he could keep an eye on her. "Don't you move from this spot. I'll be as quick as I can."

"Aren't you going to ask me what kind of clothes I want you to get me?"

Matt sighed. "I don't think I'll have much of a choice."

"Heels. Get me a nice pair of high-heeled shoes, and as for the color, it'll depend on the dress—"

Matt held up his hand. "Stop. I wouldn't buy you a pair of high heels even if I could, which I can't see being an option anyway. Or likely anything else you're about to ask me for. So don't bother. It's my money, you know. You'll have to make do with what I choose for you."

Page folded her arms and frowned. "Well, what are you standing around dawdling for? I need *some* clothes. And before I freeze to death."

Matt shook his head as he opened the door to the tinkle of chimes. He didn't want to leave her out there alone, but he couldn't imagine what a clerk or shopkeeper might make of Page in her present condition.

His eyes scanned the entire shop in a few moments. He flipped through the meager selection as rapidly as he could until he came across a quadruple extra large sweatshirt with a picture of the Montauk Point lighthouse. Then he grabbed a pair of one-size-fits-most beach sandals. It was all about as far from the dress and heels Page wanted as possible.

He took his treasures up to the quaint wooden counter that served as the checkout. He nodded at the sweet, gray-haired old lady who sat there ready to talk his ear off no doubt. He didn't want to be rude, so he pre-empted her.

"I'm sorry, but my girl is getting impatient, and I'd rather not keep her waiting." Matt tossed three twenties on the counter. "Keep the change."

He breezed out the door and found Page had already disappeared despite the short time he'd been inside the shop. His head swiveled in every direction looking for the red hair. He spotted her right away—as she was being led off toward town by a uniformed police officer. *Blast.*

"Page!" He walked fast toward them, but didn't run. They both looked suspicious enough as it was.

The man glanced back, keeping one hand firmly around Page's arm. "You know this young lady?"

Matt slowed and nodded to the officer as he approached the two of them. "I do. She was supposed to be waiting for me."

The policeman squinted at him, then looked to Page. "This man hasn't abducted you or anything, has he?"

Page frowned. "Well, I suppose you could say that he did kidnap me."

The officer frowned himself, and he kept a firm grip on Page's upper arm while his other hand hovered over his holstered weapon. *That's a relief.* As bad as the circumstances might appear, the policeman wasn't being hasty—he was glancing back and forth between the two of them and taking in every detail. That was good, too.

He addressed Page again. "In what *way*, miss?"

Matt spoke up before she could say more. "She got herself banged up, as you can see, officer. I've got a doctor friend, and I took her to the clinic he works at." It was so easy to make up a story when it happened to be the truth. "She took off from there, but I don't think she intended to come here. I doubt she knows what she wants."

Page glared at him. "I want the clothes you said you'd be getting me." She glanced around at the still and empty morning as if every eye was on her. "As for where I want to go—I want you to take me into Manhattan. If you *can*."

Matt nodded. "That's easy enough. Wherever you want to go." He gave the officer a meaningful look and kept nodding. The man gave an almost imperceptible nod in return. Page looking like an escaped mental patient might be what kept them both from being detained by the local authorities.

Matt held out the sweatshirt and sandals. "Put these on so the nice officer doesn't have to arrest you for indecent exposure."

The officer released her and watched as she accepted her new clothes with a pout. "Is this the best you could do?"

Matt took a deep breath to contain his annoyance. "That sweatshirt is the largest they had. It's big enough to fit you like a dress, and be at least a little modest. And you're welcome to buy yourself some high heels whenever you can, but with those sandals at least you won't be going around in your bare feet."

The officer sighed and gave Matt a commiserating smile. "Well, I'll let you take care of her, then."

Matt offered a weak smile of his own in return. "Thank you for your concern, Officer."

"Have a nice day, sir." He tipped the brim of his hat at Page. "Mam."

With that, the man ambled away, casting the occasional glance back. But Page was worth a glance. *Or three.*

Only once the policeman had disappeared from view did Matt place his hand to his brow to check that he wasn't drenched with sweat. His skin was bone dry, and cold.

By that time, Page had pulled the sweatshirt on and was glaring at him again. "This 'dress' is like wearing a big bag. It makes me look shapeless." She slipped on the sandals. "These do nothing for me."

"They protect the soles of your feet." He looked at said feet and the slender legs attached and took another deep breath. "*I* think that outfit does wonderful things for you." Seeing her continued glare, he hurried on. "You can find clothes more to your liking in Manhattan. You really want to go?"

"I said so, didn't I? I need to go to the bank and get some money."

"If only it was that easy. You need an account." *And money in it.*

"I do have an account. Sort of."

Of course it would be something complicated. He only hoped she knew what she was talking about, and that if she *did* have trouble she would let him know so he could help. Before she landed them in more hot water.

"Well, the LIRR begins around here. It'll take the two of us straight into Manhattan. But I really think we should find you some more clothes before we get on the train, and especially before we get into the city. You still look rather—" Matt was unsure how to phrase what he had to say in a way which wouldn't offend her.

"Underdressed," suggested Page.

Matt nodded. "At least you're safe enough now to go in and choose clothes for yourself." *And have only yourself to blame for whatever you end up with.* "So let's find some shop where you can at least get a pair of pants and not draw the wrong kind of attention." But she *would* draw attention—wherever she went, and whatever clothes she was wearing.

Page finally smiled. "I'd like that."

Matt hoped he had enough money for what she *did* find. "We still need to have that long talk about who you are, and where or when you come from and what the blazes is the deal with this watch."

"I'm not really supposed to talk about it."

"You already have." Matt stuffed the watch into his jeans pocket and steered Page down the street to where he hoped to find a clothing store.

"While it's not a hard and fast rule, we shouldn't reveal ourselves. None of our rules are rigid. We're meant to use our own good judgment."

Good judgment? Matt wondered if they knew Page well when they suggested that one.

She walked beside him, sandals flopping. "Like when I asked that nice officer what year it was. So now I know. Too."

Matt smiled to himself. No wonder the man so readily had bought into the idea of Page as a mental case—she not only looked the part, she acted it.

Matt glanced at her and nodded. "So now you know we *did* travel into the past. A lot of scientists don't even think that's possible, but I disagree, and now I know I'm right. I even think I understand the reason those rules of yours aren't hard-and-fast."

Page looked up into his face with interest. "How can you understand? I don't really myself."

"Well, mathematically speaking, traveling into the future or the past is exactly the same thing. You should appreciate that."

"My kind of math is statistical modeling of human behavior. I don't do physics."

"Oh." Matt looked down at the side of her face as she squinted into the wind. Page didn't look like she was from another world, but in a very real sense she existed in a completely different universe from him. "Anyway, the presumption that it's impossible to travel backward in time is based on the paradox principle—that if you changed anything in the past, you'd have created a paradox, which couldn't happen, so you can't travel into the past."

She yawned. "But you can. We have."

"Exactly. You prove the presumption unfounded." Matt wondered if this was so commonplace in her time that she simply couldn't be bothered with the science. "There are a couple fundamental theories that try to explain how travel into the past might be possible. One is the concept of multiple realities, with every change made in the timeline creating a new, separate branch of reality. Different from the 'old version' of events—before someone went back and changed history."

"And the other theory?"

"The one I prefer, because it makes more sense to me. Well, mathematically—" he winked at Page, "the past and the future aren't different. That's just a function of our limited perception. The past is as to-be-determined as the future, and the future has already happened just as much as the past."

Page frowned. "That makes my head hurt."

"It did get a hard knock." Matt grinned. "But that's probably why most people don't like to think about time travel that way—it's too difficult for our minds to conceive. Our brains, our natural senses, aren't designed to experience time properly. That shortcoming keeps us from being able to fully understand the implications of the math."

She shook her head as he led her onto a quiet, idyllic street filled with quaint shops. He could use this as an illustration.

Matt stopped where they stood and tried to explain. He pointed at a fashion boutique. "For you, buying whatever clothes you get in that shop is in your future—it hasn't happened yet and you can choose the clothes you want." *That I can afford to pay for.* "But three years in the future, if I'd come here, whatever clothes you're going to buy would already have been sold, even though you have yet to pick them out here in the past."

Page took a deep breath and sighed. "And now my head hurts even more. Let's go get those clothes you were talking about." She gave him a little smile as she started for the store. "But as it happens, that sounds an awful lot like the way the professor tried to explain time travel to us."

Matt smiled to himself and followed her into a small, scented shop. This really wasn't the place to find inexpensive clothes. Not that Page was looking for cheap, but they were limited to what Matt could pay cash for, and here his funds wouldn't go far. He would have to restrain Page from picking out whatever she wanted.

Her eyes lit up as she saw the array of slinky, spiked high heels displayed on pedestals.

He hated to disappoint her, but she'd get them into enough trouble without wearing those things. He checked the price on some black leather boots.

Page came and looked over his shoulder at the boots he held. "I don't want those, I want—"

"These are more practical. See, they have a nice two-inch heel—you'll like that. But it's a nice broad heel instead of a stiletto. This will give your ankle more support as well. I'm the one looking after you, and I don't want you toppling over again."

Page grabbed the boots and inspected them at length. "They *are* nice. I guess they'll do."

He would have to disappoint her again, because after paying for those boots, he wouldn't have much left. She'd have to make do with the cheapest pair of jeans they could find, no matter how unfashionable. He mentally braced himself for the onslaught.

"Once we get you a pair of these in the right size and you pick out some cheap jeans, we can go to the train station. When you get to Manhattan and have your own money to spend you can choose whatever clothes you want."

"And then we can go back to the year two thousand. Me to find my helpers, and you to your own life."

Matt managed a smile. "One thing at a time." *First I'll worry about getting her safely back to the city.* Then he could worry about the difficult dilemma he would find himself facing.

Chapter 6

Three Blind Mice

June 30th, 1997 The Upper West Side

SAM stared at the beautiful broad road with its line of trees down the center and the heavy traffic flowing in both directions. The park was gone, and her tears were drying. The surroundings of the previous moment had been replaced by rows of old but well kept apartment buildings. She'd no idea what area of the city she'd landed in, but she didn't care. She had only one thing on her mind. *Kirin.*

Though she couldn't see the woman anywhere, Sam must've been caught up in Kirin's Travel field, despite not being in range. She didn't know how it had happened, but she didn't care about that either. What concerned her was finding the fugitive.

Sam figured the same thing that had separated them all in the first place must've happened again. She checked her watch to find out the day and the year and confirm that she was at least still in New York City. Then she looked at the locator screen.

The red bar indicated a leader device—presumably Kirin with Harold's watch—somewhere to the east. The same direction Sam had been looking in when she saw the woman Travel. But Kirin had not yet escaped justice.

As long as Sam stayed in the same time as her quarry, she would continue to pursue the murderess. But Sam's ankle was still swollen and the pain had become so great she could barely stand—finding Kirin and a way to bring the woman to account was going to be tough.

Her right leg already growing tired of bearing her full weight, Sam limped over to the side of the nearest building. She sighed and let herself slide to the pavement. She let her mind drift and tried ignoring the pain, enough to get a moment of rest.

With the problems she'd already encountered, she hoped they'd been right about the devices needing twenty-four hours to recharge before they could be used for Traveling again. She would need that time to find Kirin and come up with a plan.

Clearly the size of the Travel field was off. Maybe that was just a margin of error thing though, the engineers using a fudge factor to try to keep anyone from getting lost in time. Sam could see it would be safer to err on the side of caution and say the range was a bit shorter than it actually was. The locator apps must've been programmed the same.

It gave her a slight advantage over Kirin. If only Sam could stay just outside the range indicated by their watches, then Kirin wouldn't be able to tell if they'd Travel together or not. The woman wouldn't have left in the first place if someone had shown up on her locator screen. She'd think no one had come through with her.

Not knowing if the other Travelers had become aware of her perfidy, though, she'd have to be wary. She'd likely keep checking her locator app to keep a safe distance. But she'd have no idea how far away another Traveler might be as long as they appeared as a red bar instead of a white blip. Or who it was.

What *Sam* couldn't know was what distance really would put her outside the range of the field. *It'll be tricky.*

She reached down to massage her ankle while she tried to think. Unless Kirin stayed a long time in one place, Sam would have a difficult time catching up with the woman. And it would only get harder the longer Sam sat on her rear end resting.

Then a couple of bills came floating down into her lap. She raised her head, but her unknown benefactor had already departed. On examination, she found herself holding two dollar bills and wondered how much taxi rides cost. While she needed to rest her ankle, she also burned to get after her quarry.

She pocketed the cash and checked her locator again. The red bar had switched from east to south-east, and she knew Kirin was on the move. *Where's the woman headed?* Sam would find out somehow.

Another bill floated into her lap, and once again a good samaritan walked on without comment. The little she had heard about this place must have been wrong. A quick look showed she'd been blessed with a twenty, and she suspected she now had enough.

She pushed herself to her feet and walked with care to the curb. She wasn't sure how this worked—she simply held the twenty in the air and waved it at the passing cabs. Sure enough one stopped on the other side of the parked cars and opened its door for her. Her resources were limited, but the money had literally fallen into her lap and she needed to move faster than her ankle would allow. She hobbled into the back of the cab and handed the money up to the driver.

"You need to go to the hospital, miss?"

Sam shook her head. "I need to go south."

"Where to?"

"I'm not sure. I'm not from around here. I don't even know what part of the city we're in." She nodded at the bill she'd handed him. "How far will that take me?"

"This is the Upper West Side. You want me to drive south for twenty bucks? That'll get you into Midtown. How's that?"

"I don't know. Please just take me south right now. Maybe I'll have a better idea where I'm going when we get closer."

The cabbie shook his head and started off down the street amid the streaming traffic and honking of horns. Sam watched her watch.

As she kept one eye on the screen, she considered her challenge. She couldn't avoid sometimes showing up in range, as a blip on Kirin's device. She had to hope the woman wouldn't check her locator screen so often that she'd realize she was still being pursued. Sam had no control over whether or how long she could maintain that advantage—what she would do was make every effort not to be seen by her target. The locator app would help keep from getting too close, assuming she managed to catch up in the first place.

Of course, Kirin had a head start. Traveling had increased the distance between them and then Sam had stopped to rest. Hopefully this taxi ride would make up some of the difference.

She glanced up to look at the city blocks passing by. "What will I find in Midtown?"

The cabbie stretched round to give Sam a good long look. He scratched his stubble with one hand while his other held the wheel, the other traffic ignored. "Lots of stuff. Mostly businesses."

Sam nodded, and the man returned his attention to his driving. This main thoroughfare turned more directly south, and after a few minutes Sam noticed the red bar on her watch shift to the east. "Sir, could you take the next left turn? Wherever that's feasible."

The man grunted again. Soon he turned down a one-way street, and before they'd gone a full block, Kirin appeared as a blip on the locator screen. Sam yelped, "Stop here! Please. This is it."

The cabbie shook his head but eased over to a space at the curb. Sam searched through the taxi's front windshield, but she couldn't see Kirin among the throng. Sam double checked her watch, then slid over to the door.

As she reached for the handle, she looked back at the driver. "This really is the place. Thank you."

"Hey, you want your change, little lady?"

She couldn't remember the long, boring lecture about tipping customs, but as the money had been gifted to her she should be generous.

She shook her head at the driver. "Keep it." She still had two dollars and that should buy some food. But first she had to find Kirin.

Sam smiled at the sad-eyed cabbie and then exited the taxi trying to keep herself small, which was easy enough. She waited until the cab pulled away before checking her locator app again. It certainly was easier to track the blip—unable to see the woman herself, she could still tell where Kirin had to be. About eighty meters to the east and moving south. Wanting to get further back from her target, closer to the edge of the range, Sam started walking slow to the next block where she turned south.

She looked back and forth between the people up ahead and where the woman's blip appeared on the watch screen. Once she had a clear line of sight she should be able to discern Kirin, even at the full hundred meters. She hobbled on three and a half more blocks before she finally saw her quarry.

Sam had stopped for a 'don't walk' sign at an intersection when she looked at the locator and then raised her head in the right direction to catch Kirin entering an edifice standing on the opposite corner. Sam drew back from the street and looked around her for a good vantage point to observe the building. *One that's just out of range.*

She ended up leaning against the side of a pizza parlor. This time she wasn't going to let herself sit down, because she needed to stay alert to watch for when Kirin exited. Sam squinted and read the discreet plaque next to the door where Kirin had gone in. *American International State Bank.* And that prompted Sam to remember.

During orientation, they'd mentioned research leaders having access to funds from a trust account the professor had set up in the eighteen hundreds. So the team leaders could get money to pay for food and lodging while conducting their research. Either the leader devices somehow gave them that access, or Kirin had wormed the information out of Harold. *Or both.*

If they'd mentioned further details, Sam hadn't been paying attention. She was interested now—because she needed to know what Kirin was doing, but also since Sam herself needed food and shelter. And she didn't think two dollars would last long.

She took in a deep breath. She'd save worrying about those things for when the time came. Right now she had enough to do, trying to keep close to Kirin until the woman settled somewhere. Though even then Sam couldn't relax her vigilance. *I've got Kirin in sight, and I can't risk losing her.*

Sam found her head starting to list to one side and her eyes growing heavy. She was beginning to drift off—her body must've been pumping out analgesics pretty hard for the pain to have abated to the extent she could fall asleep.

She scrambled to check the locator screen. The red bar still indicated her target to the southeast—

without knowing if her attention had wandered to the point she might have missed Kirin, she'd have to assume the woman remained in the bank.

Pinching herself to stay alert, Sam started to stretch. She glanced briefly at the faces of the people walking past and took note of the buildings all around, and she saw plenty of restaurants—it was starting to make her hungry.

She also saw the crew cut topping the tall, tightly muscled form standing at the intersection to the south, getting ready to cross over to the bank when the light turned. The man must've thought he was tracking Page. Sam stepped toward the curb, ignoring the protest from her ankle, and quickly checked her watch to see the blip appear, confirming Kirin was still inside the bank and not moving. Then Sam stretched as high as she could manage and started to yell. The pain helped.

"Bailey!" She cried out. "Bailey," she shouted again, waving her arms high above her in the hope he might actually see her.

"BAILEY!"

She watched Bailey turn his head in her direction and stand motionless as the light changed and the crowd surged forward and around him. She saw the man drop his gaze and knew he was checking his locator screen. He looked over at the bank and then back at her. And still he didn't move.

"Bailey!" She waved her arms vigorously, beckoning him over, even though the effort cost her in increasing pain.

The man gave the bank another glance. Then he stepped over to the edge of the crosswalk leading to her side of the street and waited for the light. When he finally got close, she saw the questions piling up behind his eyes.

Bailey looked around at the people passing and ignoring them both, before returning a hard stare to her. "Samantha, right?"

Sam hobbled backward to the pizza parlor and leaned against its wall once more, taking some of the pressure off her ankle. "Call me Sam. I know we only spoke briefly during orientation, but you're a sight for sore eyes."

Bailey moved up closer to her and lowered his voice. "What's wrong with your ankle? Why are you waiting way over here? For Harold? I don't understand—I thought I was tracking Page."

Sam shook her head. "It's not Harold or Page. It's Kirin in there with the leader device."

Bailey took a step back and frowned. He must have sensed something was wrong, because his eyes were troubled. "Perhaps you'd better tell me what's going on."

Sam lowered her voice to match his. "Harold is dead, murdered. Kirin stabbed him in the heart and took his watch. I managed to chase her for several blocks, but she outran me and got outside the field range. She Traveled but somehow took me along."

Bailey squinted and waited until she'd finished. Then he looked down at her ankle. "You need medical attention."

Sam bristled. "What I need is to keep following that murderess until I figure out a way to bring her to justice for killing Harold." She wanted help for her ankle, but this was more important.

"Not your job, Sam. Let the professor take care of Kirin."

She looked into his eyes and allowed the building tears to push through, pleading. Then it hit her. "You were in enforcement, weren't you? Before you joined the project. If anybody should be taking care of Kirin, it should be you."

Bailey kept shaking his head. "That's not who I am anymore. Besides—"

"I'm the only witness. And Harold's body is in the future."

Bailey's head stopped and his hard eyes looked directly into hers. "The future..."

Sam nodded. "None of the evidence even exists yet. The authorities of this time don't have a crime to investigate, and the police in two thousand don't know where to look, and even if they did..." She let her words trail off, her mind caught on something.

"By the way, how did you get here?" It was ridiculous to think this man might be in league with Kirin. *Wasn't it?*

Bailey spoke low and clear. "I just don't know." He shifted around to lean against the wall, right by her side, slouching down and fixing his gaze on the bank across the way. *He says he's not an enforcer anymore, but he's acting like one.*

"None of the others were around when I arrived, so I checked my locator app and started off toward the nearest leader. The direction was switching and I was wandering inside Central Park when suddenly I Traveled. Next thing, I was on Madison Avenue."

"Central Park?"

"A giant park in the middle of the city. It seems it was a den of iniquity and violent crime."

Sam furrowed her brows in thought. "Kirin had just gone into this big park when she Traveled. You must've been close to her."

Bailey frowned. "She didn't show as in range."

"I was outside of her range, too. The Travel field must extend farther than what the locator screens show."

"Makes sense. And it would mean—"

"That she doesn't know she brought either of us with her, and if we can stay just outside range, she couldn't be sure she's being followed. Any Traveler might be in the same time period." Sam had already thought this through. "Even if she suspects something, as long as we don't get too close she couldn't know she'd take us along with her when she Travels —if she does."

Sam paused for breath. *And Kirin doesn't know there are two of us.* "But right now she must be in there getting the money out of the trust."

Bailey shook his head. "She can't. Not the principal, not even the professor could do that. At best she has limited access to the interest."

Sam rolled her eyes. This kind of thing was why she hadn't bothered to pay attention in orientation. "Interest?"

He looked at her funny, probably thinking she was a complete idiot. *I'm not, though.*

"Money making money. That's why she'll need to Travel again. If she was willing to commit murder, she won't be satisfied with the stipend allotted for expenses. She'll want more, and that will mean Traveling further into the past, to make the money multiply."

Sam had been grateful to find she wasn't alone. She was even happier for help in her quest for justice. And she was thrilled that she'd be getting the assistance of a former enforcer who understood the way criminals operated.

Before, she had simply burned with indignation at what Kirin had done. Now Sam had hope.

She was about to ask Bailey for a fuller explanation, because she still didn't understand what Kirin was supposed to be doing, when the woman exited the bank with a pair of big suitcases. "There," Sam whispered, standing. "What took her so long?"

Bailey stayed slouching low against the wall. "I imagine she needed to make sure she got old bills."

Sam kept from looking directly at Kirin, afraid that the woman would feel the fire in her eyes. "It takes twenty-four hours for the devices to recharge for Traveling. I heard that much at least."

"It'll probably take her longer than that to prepare for the past."

"Then she'll be looking for somewhere to stay. And food."

Bailey must have heard something in her voice, because he turned and looked at her with concern. "You're injured—you need good rest, proper nutrition, and medical attention."

Sam shook her head. "No one ever died from a sprained ankle. And I've picked up two dollars—we can get some food after we know where that woman is headed."

Bailey sighed, but he didn't argue. "We'll have to be careful. One of us can keep an eye on Kirin, and the other on their locator screen."

Sam nodded. He really would be helpful. "The one checking their watch can make sure we stay on the right side of the range. That should keep us far enough away to be less visible, too."

"We'd better get moving then." He looked down at her ankle. "You don't need to be walking on that." He must have seen she was about to object, because he hurried on. "I'll carry you on my back. It'll give your ankle a rest, and the height to see the target. I can focus on getting us through the city and keep an eye on the locator screen at the same time."

Sam swallowed her protest. His plan did make sense, and she wanted to save insisting on her own way for when it mattered. And she did need to rest her ankle. "Alright."

She watched Kirin standing at the curb outside the bank as Bailey hunkered down in front of Sam so she could throw her arms around his neck and her legs around his torso. The man was hard as a rock, but this was far preferable to putting weight on her ankle. A long black car pulled up, and the driver got out to open the door for Kirin and help her with her luggage.

Seeing this, Sam leaned her head down to whisper loud in Bailey's ear while he still squatted. "Stay down." Kirin slid into the back seat of the automobile, without taking any apparent notice of them. "I don't have money for a taxi to follow her."

"In this traffic I doubt she'll get that far ahead of us. But you'd better be the one to keep an eye on the locator and give me directions. I'll make better time that way."

Sam nodded, even though Bailey couldn't see it. He waited until the car had made its way past them before he stood up and started forward. She looked down over his shoulder at her watch face. Kirin was moving fast enough that soon they'd only have her general direction.

Bailey plowed through the other pedestrians in their way with ease. Still, they'd have fallen too far behind if the hired car had carried her any real distance, instead of only a few blocks. Kirin alighted in front of an expensive hotel and lugged her suitcases in herself.

Sam watched the familiar black hair disappear through the glass doors into the lobby and knew the woman would stay. Sam thought it was a shame she wouldn't see how Bailey would last if they'd had to keep going. *Another time.*

She leaned down so he could hear her. "Stop. I saw her go into that hotel." She pointed. "Now we just need to find a good spot to wait."

He stopped and checked his own locator screen. "Not too close, not too far away and not right across from the entrance. She likely won't head out again anytime soon, but at least we know she can't Travel until the morning. I could take you to a clinic, then I could come back and watch."

Sam shook her head. "I don't want to leave, but I am getting hungry."

Bailey looked around for a minute. "There's a quiet patch of wall where I could set you down while I go grab us some food."

"That sounds like a great idea." She stuffed her two dollars into his shirt pocket. "Take your time. We want to make that stretch as far as possible."

When they reached the spot, she slid down his back to the pavement and sat up against the brick façade. She nodded at him and he was on his way.

Sam sighed. They might have to wait for days and no money for a room. *At least it's summer.*

Not to mention she now had an ally whose specialized knowledge and experience would help her come up with a way to catch Kirin.

Chapter 7

The Banker's Tale

June 30th, 2000 Midtown Manhattan

ANYA stood on the sidewalk staring at the discreet exterior of the American International State Bank as her helpers clustered close around her. She didn't think it would be a good idea for all four of them to go tramping in there together. Since she expected it to be more difficult than it should be. So far everything else had been a trial.

She turned to Tate. "I want to take someone in with me, for support, but I want to take Turner. His presence might make things go more smoothly."

Tate nodded in understanding. "Indeed. Nye and I can wait out here." He rubbed his bald pate and looked around as if wondering where.

Anya's gaze swept along the nearby buildings, stopping on the pizza parlor sitting across the street. Pizza couldn't be much different in the past. "You two can wait there. Once Turner and I have finished our business, we'll all have lunch." She was already feeling a bit weak from lack of food and hoped they wouldn't be kept long at the bank.

Nye piped up, her face red with indignation and her eyes blazing behind her glasses. "Wait in a pizza parlor, but without any money? And no telling how long you'll be in the bank while we just sit around?"

Anya sighed. "Until we get some money, none of us can eat. What else could you do but wait?"

"I can start doing my research. We're right here in my field of study. I could make some preliminary notes." Nye smiled, delivering her coup de grace. "And just sitting and doing nothing is a waste."

Tate looked at Anya. "That's true. I'd rather not be idle when we could do *something.*"

Anya shook her head. "We have too many problems for you to start researching now. You'd just get interrupted."

Turner spoke up in his clear, quiet voice. "That doesn't mean there's nothing productive they could be doing while we're in the bank—which might be a long time."

Anya hoped to take care of her business in short order, but Turner did have a point. "Well, once we have finished with the bank—and eaten—we'll want to start looking for a home base in the country. And find a way to leave messages for the other Travelers to help them find us. You could help by finding out some of the things we'll need to know to do that."

She worried about Nye and her tendency to get sidetracked, but as long as Tate was with her, hopefully the girl wouldn't get into too much trouble. "I think you two could start looking at least. And since information's free, you can do that now."

Nye's mouth looked a little sullen, but her eyes were shining with victory. "I guess it's better than sitting around doing nothing."

Anya turned to Tate, and the two exchanged a look full of meaning. "Help Nye. And be sure to be back before the pizza's all gone."

That should be enough motivation for Tate and possibly even for Nye. The girl would likely focus on her own research, but perhaps she'd end up accomplishing something related to the task at hand. *Just as long as she comes back safe.*

Anya was used to taking responsibility for these people, but without the professor now to lean on for support, she worried more than ever.

"Okay, let's do this." With a last warning look at Tate and Nye, Anya grabbed the handle and opened the door. Turner followed her through another door and into the bank's lobby.

First she noticed the incredibly clean, cool air. Then she saw the restrained but lush appointments, the quietly luxurious furniture. Anya had difficulty believing banks had been this elegant. She couldn't wait to see what other misconceptions she would be disabused of. *By the reality.*

She stepped onto the gorgeous carpet of deep reds and browns and blues and looked around for help. Turner standing tall at her shoulder should be drawing someone to them. Hopefully help.

She spotted a security guard standing discreetly next to a potted palm, ignoring them. Then she saw a young woman in a conservative skirt suit who was sashaying her way in their direction. Since she did *not* seem the type to walk like that normally, Anya presumed it was Turner's effect on the poor woman.

"May I be of any assistance?"

Anya certainly hoped so. "We're here about the Travelers' Trust."

The woman narrowed her eyes and nodded her head and straightened her spine. She wore a small gold pin on her jacket that named her Verity, which was a nice name, but a difficult one to live up to. "If you could please follow me, I'll show you where you can be comfortable while you wait."

She turned and led them across the lobby to an unmarked door of heavy oak. She opened it, waving them inside. Anya watched her give Turner a long,

considering look. Of course, that was nothing unusual. *You're wasting your time, Verity.*

Inside, plush chairs sat arranged around a long
oval table. *Very nicely polished.* Anya took a seat
for herself and plopped into it, and Turner followed
her lead. Only more gracefully.

"This is our conference room." The woman was
standing in the doorway with her hand on the knob.
"May I get you any refreshments?"

Anya tried not to show her surprise. Then she
thought of Tate and Nye, who certainly wouldn't be
so well treated, wherever they were now. She started to shake her head, but Turner spoke up first.

"That would be lovely. We could both use some
water. And maybe a little something to nibble on, if
you have it."

The woman nodded with a slight smile on her
face and closed the door behind her.

Turner squinted at Anya. "If this takes a while,
we'll need to keep up our strength. What now?"

Anya shook her head at him, but she wasn't going to argue. She'd noticed a pen and a pad of paper
on the table, but continued to look around the room
for a long moment. She'd just have to hope no one
was secretly observing them. She could at least save
giving Turner any explanations until they had more
privacy. In case someone were listening in, as im-
probable as that seemed.

She grabbed the pad and pen and held them in her lap, then pushed a button on her watch to scroll through until she reached the resources screen. She selected the current date and hit the account key.

The screen then displayed a twelve-digit alpha-numeric code, which Anya carefully copied onto the top sheet of paper. She tore that off and folded it. Then she removed the next few sheets and stuffed them into her skirt pocket.

She found herself grinning at Turner. "Can't be too careful."

Several minutes passed before someone came, and then it wasn't Verity with the refreshments she had promised, but a slim middle-aged man wearing a three-piece suit and tie and a deferential manner. The buildings and the clothes might've changed, but Anya recognized a banker when she saw one.

The man cleared his throat. "My name is Hem-mings—the branch manager. I hope you'll excuse the precaution, but though you mentioned the Trav-elers' Trust, I'd appreciate it if you could state your business more specifically."

Anya nodded. "I'm here for the Travelers' Trust stipend, as an authorized recipient. I wish to set up a subsidiary account and withdraw certain funds, in accordance with the terms of the trust."

Hemmings nodded twice. "Yes. Well." And he coughed. "You realize you'll have to prove..."

"Certainly." Anya handed him the folded over sheet of paper. "Today's access code."

The banker took the paper gingerly and nodded again. "I'll have to confirm with our records. That could take a little while. Are you comfortable?"

"Perfectly. Thank you."

The banker essayed a little bow and backed out of the conference room, closing the door as he went. Clearly he already believed they were who they purported to be. That should speed things up. Which was good since Anya was getting hungry.

The image of a pizza pie revolved around inside her mind until the Verity woman returned. She had a tray with two bottles of water, a couple of glasses and a small bucket of ice—as well as a plate spread with crackers and an assortment of cheeses, and a small dish filled with black olives.

She essayed a little smile at Turner. "Please enjoy this small repast. With compliments from Mr. Hemmings."

They waited for her to leave before saying grace ↓(9) and falling upon the vittles with enthusiasm. Anya spared some sympathy for Tate and Nye as the food disappeared. They both started guzzling the water, not bothering with the glasses or the ice. *They keep this place as cold as a refrigerator anyway.*

Having finished what little had been provided, Anya leaned back in her chair and sighed. "Do you think they waited until they were sure who we were before bringing that?"

Turner smiled. "We could have been anybody, so I don't blame them if they did."

Anya leaned forward and folded her hands together on top of the table. "I just worry about Nye. I hope they don't get lost out there. It's a big city."

Turner rolled his eyes. "They can use their locator apps to home in on you, so they can't get lost. Or you can track them down the same way."

"I know, but I had to track you all down once today. I don't want to have to do it again. I can't stop worrying what Nye might get it in her head to do. I fret about the others—what trouble might they be in and we wouldn't even know?"

"Just relax. We'll find a way to leave them messages—it's the only thing we *can* do. It'll all work out."

Anya shook her head. If only it were that easy to just stop worrying. She also had to concern herself with how much cash she'd need to withdraw to take care of immediate expenses. And how they'd manage to find and acquire a base of operations in the country without legal identification, or find a way to leave those messages. But she couldn't start solving those problems yet.

Not without the benefit of the research Tate and Nye were supposed to be starting.

Anya kept checking her watch and saw sixteen minutes pass before Mr. Hemmings returned with the Verity woman on his heels holding a memo pad with pen poised.

The banker didn't bother to sit down. "Everything checked out, Ms.—"

"Anya."

Mr. Hemmings gave a small start at hearing her name but recovered quickly. "You're the first recipient to come forward this year. The only one so far, I mean." The banker coughed. "I only meant to inform you that, as no one else has yet come forward, currently the entire yearly stipend is available. How much of those funds will you be requiring?"

"All of it." Anya looked to make sure her words were being taken down. "Twenty thousand in cash, and the remainder transferred to a subsidiary account."

The banker blinked. He clearly wished to make a remark, but his training held. He composed himself before he spoke. "Excuse me. I don't know your circumstances, but that's a sizable amount of cash to carry around. If there's some other way..."

Anya sighed. Mr. Hemmings was fond of trailing off his sentences. "We'll need cash on hand for expenses—food, transportation, and lodging."

The banker nodded while she spoke. "Yes, yes. But you won't need to carry cash. We can get you a credit card—and once your account is established, we'll provide you with an ATM card. Since this is a Friday, it'll be Monday, or possibly Tuesday before we'll have those ready. We'll need to see some identification. And have you fill out a few forms."

Anya sighed. The man was going to be difficult. "No, Mr. Hemmings. Perhaps you aren't intimately acquainted with the terms of the trust, but I most certainly am. None of that will be necessary, and we don't want to wait for those cards." They certainly wouldn't be taking any line of credit, whatever the man said. "We won't be showing you any identification or filling out any forms."

The man squinted. "I'm familiar with the terms of the trust, but understand that there are laws and banking regulations we have to adhere to."

"That prevent you from honoring your legal obligations to the trust? Your bank acts as executor." Anya stared calm and steady. She'd keep repeating herself if she had to.

"We have to comply with—"

"The terms of the trust for which you're trustees—terms that stipulate recipients only need to provide the proper access code. And a fingerprint. For future access to the subsidiary account."

"Thumbprint, yes. But—"

"The trust is a non-profit organization, and the funds are for financing research. It's not a personal or business account." Anya took a deep breath and said in a firm voice. "I'm sure you'll be able to figure out how to reconcile honoring the terms of the trust with whatever other obligations you might have."

Mr. Hemmings sighed. "Excuse me, I'll have to get authorization from the Head Office. And talk to our lawyer." At least the man wasn't going to argue any more. "And since you can't wait for a card, may we provide the bulk of your withdrawal in travelers cheques? They can be replaced if lost or stolen."

Anya nodded her assent. "That would be convenient, as well as appropriate."

The banker turned to Verity. "Ms. Dervan, prepare eight thousand in travelers cheques when you process the withdrawal, and give them the remainder in cash. And don't forget the thumbprint."

Mr. Hemmings nodded again at Anya and left. Probably to go put the responsibility for what he'd been forced to do onto someone else's shoulders.

Verity closed her memo pad and looked at both Anya and Turner. "As neither of you appear to have anything suitable for carrying around the amount of cash and cheques I'll be giving you, I have a suggestion. While we have some rather utilitarian sacks, I could find you something less noticeable. Nicer."

Anya smiled at the woman, presumably a secretary. "I'd appreciate that, I'm sure. How about if I trust your judgment about what would be proper?"

The woman nodded. "A nice bag. Large enough for your withdrawal, and that will go with your outfit. The cost will be deducted from your account."

"By the way, should we address you as Verity or Ms. Dervan?"

The corners of the woman's mouth twitched. "I do have more than one name, it's true. Now, I need to go get the kit for taking your thumbprint before I proceed with the rest."

At Anya's nod, Ms. Dervan backed out, closing the door behind her and leaving them alone again.

Turner waited patiently. Anya less so—as she found herself checking her watch repeatedly. She saw that Tate and Nye had moved beyond the range of the locator screen, somewhere to the east. *Why did no one think to program it to indicate distance as well as direction?*

While they waited, Anya made a special request to Turner. "Did you notice the way Mr. Hemmings reacted when he heard my name?"

Her helper nodded. "It seems he'd heard it before—but in what context?"

"Surely it must've been related to the Travelers' Trust in some way. I wonder if you could find out? Not from the banker, but from Ms. Dervan."

Turner smiled weakly. "I can try."

Though it seemed like a long time, only several minutes had passed before the secretary returned.

She carried a small kit which she set down on top of the conference table with care. She took the seat on the other side of Anya from Turner and opened the kit to remove an inkpad and white card. "This will only take a minute."

Anya followed Ms. Dervan's instructions, pressing her thumb onto the inkpad and rolling it slowly across the space indicated on the card. She'd have to wash her thumb before she ate again. Before she could think about when and where to do that, Ms. Dervan was handing her a small towelette, premoistened to wash with. The woman was efficient *and* considerate.

She glanced back and forth between Turner and Anya. "Now, I'll see about your withdrawal and that bag. Would you also like me to make any reservations for you? A hotel?"

Anya nodded. She hadn't really thought about that yet, her mind too full of pizza, but they would need somewhere to stay while making plans. With no idea how long that would take. "Is there somewhere close that would be suitable for us? Nothing too extravagant."

"One room or two?"

"There are four of us. Two men and two women. We'll want two separate rooms, one for the men and one for the women, with two beds in each. If that's possible."

The secretary smiled. "Certainly it's possible." She turned and sashayed her way out, without closing the door behind her this time.

They waited another twenty minutes before Mr. Hemmings returned. He announced that he'd resolved all difficulties and the funds they'd requested would be withdrawn as specified, with the remainder transferred into a subsidiary account in Anya's name. He also told them Ms. Dervan would handle all of that. The banker was needed elsewhere.

Less than ten minutes later the secretary came in carrying a large canvas tote bag in her arms. She brought it to Turner, but spoke to Anya. "The cash and cheques are on the bottom with your receipts. I took the liberty of putting a couple of newspapers on top to discourage curiosity. Sign the cheques right away, and put those receipts in a safe place as soon as you can."

Anya smiled. "That's quite considerate of you, Ms. Dervan. We appreciate it, don't we Turner?"

"Indeed." Her helper smiled at Verity and took the bag from her arms.

The secretary took a deep breath and turned to Anya. "I printed out the reservation confirmation." She reached into the inside pocket of her suit jacket and pulled out a folded sheet of paper. "Just show this to the desk clerk, and he'll take care of you. It's only a couple blocks away."

Anya reached to take the paper. "Thank you."

"I'll have your account set up this afternoon. I can call when the papers are ready, or I could come and drop them off at your hotel?" The woman darted her eyes at Turner. *They can't help it.*

"What about this ATM card thing?"

"I'll order it this afternoon, once I've set up the account. But as Mr. Hemmings said, it might take until Tuesday. Monday at the earliest."

"Well then, why don't we wait until everything's ready, and we can collect it all at one time."

Ms. Dervan gave Anya a long, considering look. "The ATM card 'thing' can be used almost anywhere to make cash withdrawals from the funds in your account. It's also a debit card that can be used many places for direct purchases. I imagine you'll find it quite useful."

It would indeed be useful. They might be stuck in the city doing research for she didn't know how long, whatever Anya wished, with no idea what their needs would be. She'd have to keep them focused on that instead of starting in on their own research. But that would only really be a problem with Nye.

This Ms. Dervan seemed to have a good understanding of what they needed, which surprised Anya—until she realized the woman must've dealt with other Travelers. The bank might already have been visited by Harold or Page in the past.

Anya doubted she'd get an answer if she asked, but at least she had primed Turner to ask the other question. She flicked her eyes to prompt him.

Turner coughed slightly, and the secretary immediately looked at him. "Excuse me, Verity. This is probably improper, but—"

Oh, dear. The poor woman probably thought Turner was getting ready to proposition her.

Ms. Dervan smiled. "Yes, Mr. Turner?"

"It seemed as if Mr. Hemmings was already familiar with Anya somehow, at least with her name. But I'm not sure I understand how that could be."

She cocked her head to one side. "I suppose it's alright to mention it. Mr. Hemmings might have, if it wasn't a moot point."

"Moot?"

"A long, long time ago, one of the trust recipients rented a safe deposit box and left instructions that we should make its contents available—to any future recipient named Anya or Page. And a couple years ago we had a Page. She took whatever might have been inside." Ms. Dervan turned to face Anya. "It's been quite a matter of speculation among the bank employees, but you can understand why Mr. Hemmings saw no need to mention it."

Anya nodded. She understood that, but her curiosity had been aroused. This was serious business that no one here at the bank *could* understand.

What was in that box? She might have greater knowledge about what she was speculating on, but she didn't have much to work with. At least Page was alright, if she'd been visiting the bank a couple years ago. Now they needed to leave the messages that would bring her back. Somehow.

Anya stood and brushed her skirt before heading for the door with Turner following, the tote bag cradled in his arms. Ms. Dervan followed him out and closed the door behind them. She spared him a fleeting glance as she strode down a hallway deeper into the bank. Hopefully with her mind back on her work, their new account.

Anya stalked straight across the lush carpet to the exit, trusting Turner to follow her out into the polluted but somehow fresher air. Glad to be out of the stifling environs of the bank, she blinked. Her eyes needed to adjust to the bright light and colors of the real world.

Then she glanced down at the hotel reservations in her hand and back up at the street signs. It would take time to orient, but she got the gist of the directions. But pizza came first.

As Turner walked with her toward the food, he asked the question still on her own mind. "What do you suppose was in that safe deposit box?"

Anya's mind seemed clearer now, and she tried to think it out as she answered. "Just as we want to find a way to leave messages for the others, it's reasonable they might try to contact us somehow. This must've been Harold's doing. Since it had been left for me or for Page. We both would have to visit the bank to get funds, so it makes some sense in its way. But it's a very limited method. One message, only into the future and for only one of two people at a specific time and place. We'll have to do better than that."

Turner nodded in agreement at her explanation as they both approached the restaurant. The lure of the pizza had quickened their steps. But she didn't see Tate or Nye waiting outside.

Turner must have felt her concern. "They could be inside. Maybe wanting to get off their feet, since they likely haven't been sitting down all this time."

Anya shook her head. She checked her locator and saw they were still east of her somewhere, and still too distant to be blips. "I'm going to go look for them. You can wait here."

"Oh, no. You're not going out there alone. I know this has been a rough day for you, so you can stay here with the—with the newspapers, while *I* go out and look."

"I'm not waiting around on my own. I'd only be worrying about you, then."

Turner carried the tote inside to an empty booth and set it down next to the wall. "Then I guess we order some pizza, and trust that Tate and Nye will arrive as soon as they're hungry enough."

"If they haven't returned by the time we've finished the pizza, we'll start searching. Together."

"If and when. We'll have to eat the pizza first." He turned his smile on a waitress approaching their table, and Anya knew they'd get great service. "Jenny," he said, glancing at her plastic nametag, "we'd like the largest pizza you can make, with everything you have to put on it."

As Jenny wrote their order on a pad, she asked, "Drinks?"

"Water will be fine, Jenny."

After the waitress had left them, Anya glanced over at the tote bag beside Turner. "Can I see one of those newspapers Ms. Dervan gave us?"

Turner nodded and reached down into the bag. He looked and searched and came out with the paper for Anya and a few bills which he casually folded and slipped into his shirt pocket. He handed her the paper with a wink. "We'll have to pay for the pizza, you know."

Anya was more than happy to let Turner handle paying the bills. "And the water?"

"It may be free. But we don't want to drink soda or beer, so it doesn't matter."

"What about iced tea?" That would be good and refreshing, especially in this heat.

Turner smiled and got up to chase down their waitress. Soon their pitcher of iced tea had arrived and not long after that a freshly baked pizza on a hot plate that took up almost the entire table.

Of course that was when Tate and Nye finally arrived. Nye bounced over and Tate followed with his arms full of newspapers that looked like they'd been having a rough time of it.

Nye beamed. "Look. The perfect way to leave those messages, and—" She stopped when she saw the paper in Anya's hand. "After we went to all that trouble digging through garbage cans."

Anya smiled. Leave it to an archaeologist to go digging through the refuse. "Now we have plenty of information to evaluate. And pizza to put away. So set those down, Tate, and help us eat."

Chapter 8
Ties that Bind

November 30th, 1998 Queens (on the (LIRR) *TB*

MATT appreciated how Page looked in those black boots and blue jeans and the gray sweatshirt, but he hadn't offered any more compliments. At least she wasn't complaining anymore, so she had to be satisfied. Indeed, she'd grown more and more pleased as the train had rattled through Queens and gotten closer to the island of Manhattan.

Early on, when the background noise was mostly the regular clacking of the tracks and squealing of wheels, when they could still hear each other, Matt had tried to converse with Page. He had needed answers to questions he wanted to ask before the train grew crowded and people could overhear.

Though most New Yorkers were adept at ignoring other people. If anyone did hear talk about time travel, they'd probably dismiss it, or consider Matt and Page to be nutcases. Which wasn't a problem. The problem Matt had was Page's refusal to discuss any of it—when she came from or what it was like.

She wouldn't discuss the future with him at all. Though she admitted it shouldn't be a problem, she wouldn't without a sufficiently good reason. Which he couldn't give her.

He'd questioned her about this time-travel device disguised as a watch, but she wouldn't give him a hint how it worked. Not even how long the thing needed to recharge. He'd had a small success when he had demanded to know how the device could recharge all on its own.

"*You* are recharging it. Matt," she'd said. "The watch draws energy from your body's own electrical field. And that's as much as I know myself."

He'd found that little detail quite interesting. *I hope I don't blow this thing's fuse.*

He'd had a little more success in getting her to talk about herself. He'd learned she'd been a coder before she had somehow gone off the deep end into fantasy math. And that she possessed a rose-tinted view of twentieth century dating, as if it were some kind of courtly romantic ritual. He'd gotten her to open up by sharing some of his own history. How he'd moved from the Midwest so he could study at GTI, but didn't care for living in New York City.

Matt hadn't progressed far, though, before she had used the excuse of the increasing crowd to shut down all conversation, leaving him with nothing to do but stare into her beautiful crystal blue eyes. She glared at him in return, making him smile and irritating her further. Which only made him grin.

Page gave up on glaring, and he watched as her gaze turned inward, the wheels turning in her mind. She was the most complicated and puzzling woman Matt had ever met, before he included the fact that she was a time-traveler from the future.

He was watching those wheels turn when he felt the passing shadows stop. He looked over and saw five slovenly dressed young men—like the juvenile delinquents who'd snatched Page's purse. Standing in the aisle way too close.

Page broke off whatever internal dialogue she'd been having with herself and swiveled her head to squint at them. These weren't the same thugs, but they were the same type—hoodlums. He wondered what she was feeling. Whatever *she* felt, he didn't care for the way they were leering at Page, or pressing in closer with hostile stares for him. *They're looking for trouble.*

Matt stood to shield Page and let his foot slip— 'accidentally' tripping one of them, who then fell backward into his friends, knocking a pair of them down like bowling pins.

"I'm so, so sorry," Matt pleaded, trying to look apologetic as he grabbed Page's hand and pulled her to her feet. "We were just leaving, and I should've watched where I was going."

The young men had started swearing, more to themselves than at Matt, but then they turned their attention to him. Their language was totally inappropriate in front of a lady.

He stepped over the legs of the three men who lay sprawled in the aisle. Turning back, he wrapped his hands around Page's hips and lifted her in the air, over the seats and the other passengers and to the far side of the aisle, putting himself between her and the delinquents. He'd lived long enough in the city to recognize gang apparel, though he couldn't identify them. It hardly mattered. They dressed the way they did so people would be afraid.

Matt saw one of the two who remained standing pull a switchblade out of his pocket. Thankfully the other decided to take a swing at him. Matt shifted a little out of the way and spun the man around, causing him to crash into his friend. *Time to get out of here.*

He pushed Page ahead of him, down the aisle and into the next car before the thugs could get up and follow. He prodded her on to the next car and glanced out to see where the train was. It would be stopping soon at the Woodside station.

Matt had managed to hustle Page through two more sections by the time the train had screeched to a halt. He continued pushing her forward into the next car, despite the difficulty of other passengers getting on and off in throngs.

Page had kept quiet until then. "Why aren't we getting off the train and away from those, those—"

Now Matt could imagine what she was feeling. "They'll expect us to get off. They think we're running because we're afraid, and scared people would be leaving the train. So we stay on."

"And we're not afraid?"

"Not of them. But I do worry about you." Matt sighed. "Let's get as far away from them as we can, though. They'll give up, and we can keep going and get you the rest of the way to wherever you're headed. Your bank, I suppose?"

Page was still being close mouthed about precisely where it was and what she'd do when she got there. She'd refused to tell him any more than what she considered he needed to know. As if she could understand what that was.

He kept them moving forward through the train as it entered the tunnel. Without pursuers though, he didn't rush—they took their time ambling along as they sped under the East River.

Once they slid into Penn Station, Page had no choice but to tell Matt where to take her. While he fought to get her off the train and through the mayhem of the bustling transportation hub, she gave up the name of the bank and its address.

It was a dozen or so blocks away, and he didn't want to spend what little cash he had left on a taxi. And stopping at an ATM, assuming his card would work, would only encourage Page to spend more of his money, so he presented her with just two alternatives. "We could walk a dozen blocks or take the subway to Forty-second and walk from there."

Page ignored him, striding through the crowd as if she knew where she was going and not paying any attention at all to her environment. It irritated him. She'd continue getting into trouble that way, and he had to keep running interference for her amid the throng.

Finally she gave him a quick glance. "The subway. We've walked enough for now, and there will be all that shopping to do later."

All the way, riding the subway and up onto the street, he focused on one thing and one thing only, making sure she arrived safe and sound. At least he accomplished that, and soon enough he was following her out of the loud, bustling city into the tasteful lobby and quiet atmosphere of the American International State Bank.

Once inside, Page stopped and stared at Matt. "I probably shouldn't have you along for this. You already know too much you shouldn't."

Matt grinned. "If I know too much as it is, then it can't hurt if I learn a little more."

Page thought about that for a moment and then nodded. "True. And I may need some help. Since it's your fault I don't have my helpers with me, you'll have to take their place, until I have them back. So, how do I go about this?"

Matt shook his head. "About what? You've got to give me more of a hint if you want my help."

"I'm here as an authorized recipient, to access funds from the Travelers' Trust."

Matt nodded, his brain already connecting the dots. Setting up a trust in the past made sense as a way to get money into the hands of time-travelers, if there was a way to get it started properly in the first place. Which someone must have done for Page to be able to know about it—probably back in the days when regulations were a lot less strict. *Amazing if it's actually survived to the present day.*

He waved his arm at what he presumed to be a customer service desk, where a young man in a nice blue suit sat behind a computer screen placed atop an antique cherry oak desk. "Let's try over here. If he can't, I imagine he'll at least know who *can* deal with a complicated issue like yours."

Matt helped Page into one of the comfortable leather chairs and dropped himself into the other. "Good morning."

"One minute, please." The young man continued tapping on his keyboard for a minute and then turned to face them—and noticed Page for the first time. "I'm terribly sorry for making you wait, miss. Now, how can I help you today?"

Page was all business. "I don't want this to take any longer than necessary. I've got shopping to do. I'm a recipient of the Travelers' Trust stipend, and I need some cash."

The young man blushed and cleared his throat. "Let me get Mr. Hemmings for you. He's the branch manager. It will only take me a moment." Then he sprang out of his chair and scurried off.

While he was gone, Matt managed to get in a quick question. "If someone went back into the past and established this trust, how are *you* supposed to access those funds?"

Page glanced around to make sure no one was watching. "I'll need the device to show you."

He shook his head. "Here, I'll hold it out, and you can do whatever you need to do with it. But I'll keep hold of the thing. As insurance."

"You still don't trust me?"

"You don't trust *me* yet. I guess we'll have to work on the whole trust thing."

Matt held the watch out low between them, so no one could see. Page stretched her fingers to push the buttons on the side of the watch and leaned in to peer at the tiny screen. He held it firmly, but all she did was move her lips as she read.

She leaned up and back into her chair. "Thank you. Matt." Her tone had bite to it, but he thought she was being sincere.

"Care to tell me what that was all about?" ·

"The bank gets a new code for each day. An app on the device generates an alphanumeric sequence to match that, based on the date and according to an encrypted algorithm."

He thought it was pretty sophisticated, but if it had all been set up far in the past, it had to be pretty low-tech on the bank's end of things. As a mathematician Page would understand how it worked. Of course, so did he.

The young man returned, followed by a middle-aged fellow who was the perfect image of a respectable banker and a smart young woman who would be his secretary. Though she wouldn't be called that.

The banker discreetly examined them both, and from the fleeting look on the man's face, Matt didn't think either of them passed muster. But his voice was pleasant enough as he introduced himself.

"I'm Mr. Hemmings, the branch manager. And you are?"

"Here for the Travelers' Trust stipend," Page blurted out without preamble. "You'll need today's access code. It's 4K—"

Mr. Hemmings held up his hands in a rush to stop her. "Not here." Though the only other people around were the secretary and the clerk. "Come to the conference room." He nodded to his secretary. "Grab your memo pad and the fingerprint kit."

Matt and Page followed him to a spacious room with a giant table and comfortable chairs. Seating themselves, they waited for the woman to turn up. As soon as she arrived with pad and pen to take it down, Page rattled off the access code.

Mr. Hemmings took the sheet his secretary tore from her notepad, folded it, and stuffed it into his breast pocket. "Now, your name please. I presume you'll want to set up a subsidiary account, and Ms. Dervan here will take your thumbprint for our records."

"My name is Page. I suppose I might as well set up the account now, for the future. But what I really need is some quick cash, so I can buy some decent clothes."

Mr. Hemmings' head had snapped up when she said her name, but he didn't blink an eye at the rest of it. "I'll leave you with Ms. Dervan while I confirm your eligibility." He turned, then walked out of the room, hopefully to do what he'd said he'd do.

The secretary took Page's thumbprint and left, leaving them alone for the first time in forever. Or that was how it felt. Trying to think what he might say, he watched Page while she sat staring into the distance. Ms. Dervan returned before he had come up with anything.

The woman ignored him completely and talked to Page. "Mr. Hemmings confirmed your access to the funds. How much are you requesting?"

"It's already late November. I'll take whatever remains of this year's stipend."

Ms. Dervan nodded. "A small portion was withdrawn earlier in the year, but the bulk of the funds are still available." She pursed her lips for a minute. "You said you needed cash for clothes shopping—I presume you'll need a sizable amount for that. How much? And the rest in your account? We'll order a debit card for you to use to access those funds."

"Nice clothes appear to be quite expensive." Her gaze drifted, and Matt knew she would be doing the math in her head, extrapolating from the prices she had seen in the one shop she'd been in. "Ten thousand should be enough. I only have today to shop— then I'll be leaving. So I won't want the debit card. Not now."

Ms. Dervan nodded with a blank face, but she seemed to understand. "I notice you don't have a purse. We can provide a bag to carry the cash in."

Page clenched her jaw. "My beautiful bag was stolen." When the secretary didn't say a word, Page continued, "I suppose it's a paper sack or something you'll put it in for Matt to carry?"

Ms. Dervan displayed an admirable lack of response. "I'd be happy to find you something nicer than that." She looked Page up and down. "There's an accessory boutique not far from here that carries a nice leather bag. Black, to match your boots. And large enough to hold the money you'll be withdrawing. Of course, the price will be deducted from the funds being made available to you."

"That sounds fine. Just see that the expense is deducted from what's going into the account, not from the ten thousand."

The secretary made a quick notation. "At any point in the future you can come back and we'll get you that debit card."

Page simply nodded.

Ms. Dervan offered a thin smile. "Then I'll see about acquiring that purse for you and taking care of your withdrawal." She started for the door. "By the way, Mr. Hemmings had something he needed to check on. I expect he'll be back to talk with you soon." And she was gone.

Matt wouldn't have minded waiting, hoping as he did for another minute alone with Page, but the banker entered soon after his secretary had left.

The man cleared his throat a couple of times before speaking. "I'm afraid this is rather unusual—" Matt could almost hear him thinking how the whole business was unusual, but the man didn't say it out loud. "As it happens, seven years ago another trust recipient rented a safe deposit box here. And gave the bank instructions that the contents of the box should be made available to any future trust recipients who happened to be named Anya or Page."

"My name is Page."

"Well, yes. Exactly. Since no Anya has yet appeared, I'm obliged to inform you about the box and its circumstances—and give you the opportunity to examine its contents. What you would do with what it contains would be up to your discretion."

Matt felt sorry for Hemmings. The man must have been burning with curiosity, between the unusual aspects of the complicated trust and now this. But it was an itch the banker would never be able to scratch. Still, it was part of the job.

Page looked at the man for a long minute. "Who left the box?"

Mr. Hemmings coughed into his hand. "I'm not at liberty to reveal that. But I might conjecture that the contents could reveal the person's identity."

"I suppose I should at least take a look inside. Can I go ahead and do that right now? Since I have to wait anyway."

The banker smiled with a little nod. "Certainly, Miss Page. I'll escort you to the vault myself." He paused and glanced at Matt.

She shook her head. "He can wait here. I think I should examine this by myself."

Matt smiled to show he didn't mind. "Alright, you go satisfy your curiosity. I have other things to occupy my thoughts."

Page's smile in return was disingenuous. She turned and followed Mr. Hemmings out, and once she'd gone Matt allowed himself a deep sigh. He'd enjoy getting out of here to take her around town, even if it was to go clothes shopping, but then she'd want to return to two thousand and find her fellow time-travelers. Back to the present, from his point-of-view, where she would leave him behind.

He pulled her watch from his jeans pocket and strapped it around his wrist and was pondering the life he would soon return to when the door opened and Page returned. Seeing the look on her face, he flew out of his chair to meet her, though he had no idea what he could do.

She was alone and white as a sheet, and in her hands she clutched an envelope and another watch like the one Matt held for her. He reached out for her hand, but she pulled back without even looking at him. He looked into her beautiful blue eyes and saw the wheels behind them were turning fast.

Matt couldn't help but wonder what had caused this reaction—if it were whatever was in that envelope, or something about that watch. *Or could there have been more in the box that she had left behind?* "Are you alright? What's wrong?"

Page shook herself, and the color suffused itself back into her face. She sat down in the chair she'd left a little while ago and took a moment before she folded the envelope with care and stuffed it into her jeans pocket. Then she focused on the watch she still held in her hands.

"This is a device similar to mine—the one you continue to hold hostage. Its capabilities are more limited though. It can't Travel on its own, but if it's within range of a leader device like mine when *it's* used for Traveling, then it develops a sympathetic field attuned to the leader. It transports the wearer along in the same field, to the same destination. Or close to it."

Matt nodded. "I suppose that means we don't have to hold on to each other for dear life when we go back to two thousand then. What's the range?"

Page almost smiled. "You're quick, I like that. But I'm not sure I should tell you—we're still working on our trust issues, remember? And we'd better stay as close as possible when we Travel. It seems that distance increases on arrival. That's how I lost my helpers when I first landed."

Matt nodded. "I noticed that when we arrived on that cliff top in Montauk, we were farther apart than when we'd left. The edge of the bluff was badly eroded. If it weren't for that separation, we'd likely both have fallen over when it crumbled."

Page dismissed that with a wave of her hand. "Even my leader device shouldn't have Traveled the two of us—the watches are only meant to transport one person." She frowned. "They're also supposed to Travel to the same physical location. I suppose you must have accidentally changed the coordinates somehow. Or maybe it was just an error caused by there being two of us and one device."

"Your time-travel devices ought to be more reliable than they seem to be. You didn't have a hand in programming them, did you?"

She glared at him. "Anyway, the point is this—you don't have to worry about being abandoned in the past anymore. I'll give you this helper device so you can be sure you'll be Traveling with me when I go. We can exchange watches now. Then when that woman brings my money we'll go shopping."

Matt started shaking his head right away. "I'll hold onto this one a little longer. I'm not sure I trust you. After all, you didn't even tell me how close I'd have to stick to you to be in range."

"Because you're my helper for now, and I don't want you to abandon me—without the range, you'll have to remain right by my side. Why would I leave *you* behind?"

He didn't want to argue. He knew *he* wouldn't abandon *Page* and he needed to make sure she kept him close a little longer. "Show me how to operate your device, and *I* can be the leader."

Page glared at him. "No. If you're going to keep my watch, you'll have to rely on me to set it for you. As long as you don't know how to use it, then I can trust you won't find a way to leave *me* behind. Another reason not to tell you the range."

Matt nodded. "Stalemate. I guess we have no choice but to stick close to each other. At least until we get back to two thousand."

"You're being ridiculous—"

He knew she would've continued the argument, but the door opened and Ms. Dervan entered. The secretary was carrying a large black leather bag. It bulged, presumably with all that cash Page intended to blow on clothes. It didn't look much like a purse to Matt. But it matched the boots he'd bought Page and was big enough to hold the money.

Page eyed the thing critically. It was classy and expensive, so it must've been the bulge she objected to. She gestured at Matt, and Ms. Dervan dumped the thing into his arms as he held them out. It clearly wasn't the weight Page didn't like, since she was having him carry it.

The secretary turned to Page. "The receipts for the cash withdrawal and the bag and your account information are in the bag, on top of the money. Is there anything else?"

Page shook her head. "That will be sufficient." She stood and gestured at Matt and walked out with him following.

He trailed after Page across the lobby and out of the bank. He would have a difficult time trying to take care of her, holding the heavy bag and keeping up as she stalked down the sidewalk.

He almost had to yell to make sure she'd hear. "Where do you think you're going? We should take a taxi. You can afford to be driven around in style now."

He really wanted her to take that taxi—it would be safer with all this money, and it would be a load off his arms as well as his mind.

Matt played his hole card. "All the nicest shops are down by Times Square. That's a long walk."

Page paused and turned to squint at him. "You might actually know what you're talking about. If you don't know anything about clothes, you should at least know enough about this city. Alright. Get me a cab." Then her eyes widened as they traveled over his shoulder. "I don't believe it."

Matt tried not to be irritated with her. "What can't you believe? An available taxi?"

She shuddered. "Those thugs from the train. The ones you tripped over."

Matt didn't bother trying to correct her. "What about them? Surely you don't mean—"

Page grabbed his arm. "They're down the street behind you, coming this way. They see us."

"They could hardly miss us." Matt fought down a flutter in his stomach. Protecting Page with arms full would be a challenge, so he tried to shift the bag onto her, where it belonged anyway. She pushed it back into his arms. "Are you sure they're the same ones? They'd have had to follow us all the way into Penn Station and on the subway and all the way to the bank. It hardly seems likely."

"Look for yourself."

Matt glanced behind him and saw the very delinquents they'd encountered on the train. That *is not good.* They must have wanted payback pretty bad to have gone to all the trouble of following him and Page across the city. Matt doubted they'd fail to understand the significance of the bulging bag he'd carried out of the bank—which would provide them extra motivation. *This is going to get ugly.*

He grabbed Page's hand with his own sticking out from under the bag. "Come on. Move."

Page stood still. "They wouldn't dare do anything here in the open with all these people around. We couldn't outrun them anyway."

Matt wondered what it would take to wake her up to the reality of life in the city. But she was right about one thing—there was no way to outrun those hoods, but he had to get her out of harm's way and there was only one way he could do that under the circumstances. He hoped the thing was sufficiently recharged.

He didn't have time to ask or to have her show him how to operate it properly. Or even let her do it herself.

As the ruffians closed in, Matt was already fiddling with the watch as he shifted the bag and tried to remember exactly what he'd done when he was playing with it in the clinic this morning.

He did the same thing again. Only this time he had his arms full of the bulky bag. He'd rather have been holding Page.

TB

Chapter 9

Partners in Crime

July 1st, 1994 Midtown Manhattan

SAM sat up against her quiet patch of wall, leaning back on the white brick and sticking her foot out far enough for her bandaged ankle to be plainly visible. She had sent Bailey out to look for food, and twenty-nine hours ago he'd returned with an explanation. Which he'd finished making by the time the woman from the shelter showed up in a taxi.

The man had usurped her observation post, and she'd had little choice but to go along with it, since it *had* been a good idea. At least she'd gotten a ride to the place. And medical attention, a hot meal, and a good night's rest. She'd made him promise though, to stick to the target and to give her a full report.

Still, she'd only agreed because of that twenty-four hour window when Kirin was unable to Travel. Sam had needed the rest, and her ankle appreciated the sprain being treated—after the way she'd handled the initial injury, it was a miracle she managed to *walk*. But she was healing so fast that she knew she'd be able to run again. *Someday soon.*

She'd risen early this morning and, taking it as easy as she could on her ankle, she'd walked several blocks following the directions on her watch. It had led her back to this same hotel, where she'd found Bailey occupying her spot and keeping an eye on his own locator. The man had at least fulfilled that part of his promise to her—he'd then proceeded to deliver on the rest.

According to him, Kirin had left the hotel soon after Sam had been driven away. He'd followed the woman over twenty blocks to a grand library guarded by two stone lions, and she'd stayed there far into the evening. He'd remained outside the building to keep from being discovered. Then he'd followed her back to the hotel without incident and taken an occasional nap in an alley down the street.

Sam had requested a fuller explanation of what he thought the woman had been up to. His theory was that Kirin was doing research at the library to discover what companies might have gone bust or gone big in the recent past.

Bailey believed Kirin was using Harold's access to the trust stipend to get seed money to take back into the past, where the research she'd done would become knowledge of the future. Which she could then use to invest her ill-gotten gains and turn them into a vast fortune. He predicted that she'd repeat her performance at the bank as she hopped back in time, stealing even more of the professor's money.

Standing there and absorbing all this, Sam had suddenly found herself alone in a section of the city called Greenwich Village—and three years further into the past. She'd used her watch to head toward Kirin and thus bumped into Bailey doing the same. At least they'd landed relatively close—to each other if not to Kirin. Sam had even let Bailey carry her all the way back to where the woman was staying at the very same hotel.

Kirin, though, had Traveled before the twenty-four hours had fully elapsed, which meant that the battery recharge time had a fudge factor, and Kirin knew it. Another complication to make chasing her more difficult.

Of course, the woman should be unaware that she'd taken stowaways along with her and that she was still being pursued. *Chalk one advantage up to the good guys.* And as long as they could maintain that advantage, they would have an opportunity to stop her. If they could figure out how to use it.

Sam flipped from the locator screen to the regular face of her watch and checked the time. A rush of afternoon pedestrians should sweep by soon, and she wondered if they'd be as generous as the lunch crowd had been.

She wished she had Bailey slumped beside her, despite the man's intransigence. She'd refused his suggestion to spend another night in a shelter, since they could no longer rely on having that twenty-four hour window. She wouldn't risk getting any further away from Kirin than she had to. He'd then insisted on going off to do some day labor to earn them some cash, leaving Sam to watch their target alone.

She'd had no choice but to let him go. At some point though, she'd have to find a way to make sure he understood who was in charge, or else he'd take control by default.

So far the man's predictions were panning out. After Bailey had departed to search for work, Kirin had left her hotel on foot. Sam had followed her to the bank and leaned against the same pizza parlor while she waited for the woman to emerge. Just as before, a hired car had arrived to carry the woman and two large suitcases away.

Sam had presumed those cases were filled with more of the money Kirin was stealing and the woman was taking it back to her hotel. *But she could do something unpredictable at any time.*

Sam had followed as best she could. The previous day, as she'd waited for Bailey's return, passersby had donated enough that she could have taken a taxi to trail Kirin, but Sam had decided to conserve her funds for a real emergency and walked.

The few blocks back to the hotel were no hardship, but though the shelter staff had properly iced and wrapped her ankle, it'd started to throb by the time she had gotten to the hotel. Confirming Kirin actually *was* inside the building, Sam had slid to the ground in the spot Bailey had usurped the day before. And been grateful for the chance to rest.

She could've bought a decent lunch when she'd begun to get hungry, but she hadn't wanted to leave her post. The benefit to sitting there looking pitiful during the lunch hour had been quite a haul in sympathetic contributions, so that when Bailey showed up at the end of the day, she might have made more than he had. *Then* she could send *him* for food.

At first it had been alright, but her hunger had gradually gnawed at her throughout the afternoon. She'd gotten up and stretched now and then, but it hadn't helped her stomach.

The work day ended and people streamed past. Her body had begun to protest in earnest, and Sam was considering a quick visit to one of the food carts the next block over when a giant shadow fell across her face.

Sam looked up to see Bailey standing there with a gyro in either hand. He smiled down at her. She reached up and grabbed one of the sandwiches and managed to tell him thanks before she began eating. He slumped down beside her and ate with his hard eyes locked on the hotel entrance. After they'd finished, he tried to hand her a wad of bills.

She shook her head. "I've got my own now, so you'd better keep that. How was the job?"

"Hard. But I've done that kind of work before. What about you? Let's hear *your* report."

"I'll tell you. Despite your attitude. It was a repeat performance from yesterday. She showed up at the bank a little earlier in the day, but that's it. Now she's holed up in the hotel."

"Exactly what I told you she'd do. And it's a holiday weekend, so she probably went early to make certain she could complete her business before they closed."

"I grant you your excellent understanding of the criminal mind." Sam crumpled her gyro wrapper into a ball and squeezed tight. "So, what's the woman been up to in her hotel all this time? It's not like we can find out, so I'll take an educated guess."

"As much time as Kirin spent at the library last night, I doubt she needs to do any more research. I imagine she's trying to turn all that cash into something more portable. It won't be practical to carry around those four suitcases everywhere. And she'll likely want to go back to the bank for more."

Sam goggled. "More? Kirin must already have more money than I'd ever know what to do with."

Bailey looked down at her with an odd expression on his face. "Maybe so. But the kind of greed that will compel somebody even to murder—it's an insatiable hunger. So I expect she intends to keep stealing more until it's no longer practical. Or until she gets bored."

Sam shook her head. She couldn't understand Kirin and that kind of desire. And for *money.* "How did she get access to the trust three years from now if she claimed as a recipient today?"

"I suspect she gave two different names. Bankers don't like to ask awkward questions, and they'd not be likely to compare thumbprints."

"Even if a woman shows up looking exactly like one from three years ago? With a different name?"

"It might make them curious, but if she had the proper access code, they would satisfy the terms of the trust and not their own personal curiosity."

Sam was skeptical, but he should know, and she had more questions for him. "She must've left the first two suitcases full of cash at the hotel. Maybe in the hotel safe as you suggested." Kirin hadn't taken the things to the bank with her. "And I can see why she wouldn't want to Travel with four of them. So what *will* be easy for her to carry around? And how will she exchange the cash for that?"

Bailey sighed. "I'm not sure. Gold or other precious metals would be less portable. Rare stamps or coins would lose their value as she traveled further into the past. Her best bet would be jewelry or gems —they'd be lightweight and small enough to carry on her person. It's what the professor took back to get the funds for starting the trust in the first place."

Sam could see Kirin collecting a lot of beautiful gems and jewelry, wearing her riches. "Why didn't she just withdraw the money in gems to begin with? Surely that would've been easier."

Bailey gave her another one of those strange expressions. "Banks don't do that. She'll need to find a dealer. A less than reputable one."

"Why less than reputable? And how would she find such a person?"

"She'll want someone who won't bat an eye at business by suitcases full of cash. As for how she'll find them, I'd wager she researched *that* last night as well. She'd only have to look in the newspapers and see who'd been arrested for fencing. Then she could deal with them in the past before they'd been exposed."

The man had proved to be right so far, and Sam knew she'd best listen to him—at least when he was giving her his expert explanations. Not necessarily when he was trying to give her advice about what to do. She would know that herself.

"Supposing you're right—how long will it take her to do whatever she has to do?"

Bailey shook his head. "I don't know how long it might take her to line up the deal, or when she'd set it up for. But I imagine it will all take place at that hotel. She won't want to take the money anywhere, and her room would be private enough for just such a transaction. It's a classy hotel that should be safe ground for both sides. Relatively speaking. Criminals don't tend to trust each other."

Sam turned her head to look her partner in the eye. "This is what's worrying *me*—" Bailey might know about Kirin the criminal, but Sam understood Kirin the woman better than he ever could. "However nice that hotel may be, if she has to stay very long, she'll want to go out and see the sights. Spend some of that money." Which indirectly touched on another sore spot between Sam and Bailey.

When she'd brought up the possibility of waylaying Kirin to get those ill-gotten gains and, more importantly, the leader device back, he hadn't even been willing to entertain the notion.

Sam had appealed to his expertise. As a former enforcement officer, he ought to have some decent ideas about how they could steal those things back. He'd claimed that his training prevented him from breaking the law himself. And that they'd no right to the money or the device themselves.

They'd argued over that while they walked back from Greenwich Village. Explaining that they had a moral obligation to stop the murderess from enjoying the fruits of her crimes had made no impression. Sam had let the subject lie, but it was an issue.

She didn't know herself what she was going to do to stop Kirin, to bring her to justice—but when the time came, Sam would need to be sure of Bailey, that he would help her.

The man was nodding. "You may be right. But since your ankle is still healing, I'll follow her if she goes out tonight."

Sam had a hard time controlling her irritation. Bailey had no business telling her what she could or could not do. She didn't challenge him at that moment. She didn't know what she'd do though, if the man tried to hinder her when she did what she had to do. Whatever that ended up being.

She made an effort to stand every hour on the hour and stretch and exercise her ankle by walking a full block. It was good therapy, and it would show Bailey what she could do. Eventually the day began to fade though, and she ceased her perambulations —if Kirin did go out, it would be at night.

Sam settled back down in her spot, but not too comfortably. Something told her tonight was it and that she needed to be ready. Even so, she drifted off into a light slumber. The two of them must've made quite a sight—Bailey's big muscular form slumped beside a small young woman sleeping on the sidewalk. While he stared at his watch.

She was awakened by her partner pushing a finger into her shoulder. "She's coming."

Sam started awake and looked first to the hotel entrance. Then she glanced down at her locator app where Kirin had appeared as a blip, meaning she'd left her room. The woman must've moved close to this side of the building. Likely she had descended to the lobby and was headed for the street. Sam had been right.

She was glad Bailey had awakened her for it— he might've left here there so he could follow Kirin on his own. *No, he wouldn't have left me alone and asleep.* But he might try to leave Sam there now.

They stood and walked further down the sidewalk to get out of range, in case Kirin happened to check her locator screen. When the woman left the hotel might be a natural time to do that, too. If she saw a blip and looked in their direction, they would lose their best advantage. Surprise.

If they lost that edge—Kirin now had the means to hop on a plane if she wanted to get away. And if the woman discovered she was still being pursued, she'd leave them so far behind they would have no hope of catching up to her before she could Travel. And that would be the end of the chase.

As soon as they were far enough away to be a bar instead of a blip, Bailey returned to keeping an eye on his watch. Sam stared across the street and tried to watch the hotel door from the corner of her eye. She still worried that Kirin would feel the heat of a direct gaze.

Her partner grunted. "There she is."

Sam shifted her head a little so she could see the woman, now wearing an elegant evening gown. At least that was the impression Sam had—the way she was looking, she could only make out a blur. Something else was different about Kirin, but Sam could not put her finger on what.

Hopefully Bailey was looking properly and saw what it was. Maybe he could also tell her how Kirin had gone shopping under his very nose. Sam's brief glimpse of the woman ended as the blur slid into yet another hired car that soon rolled away.

Sam snorted. "Your surveillance last night left something to be desired. Since she managed to buy a dress without you noticing."

"Or she bought it at a shop inside the hotel. Or their concierge service is really good."

Not that good, surely. "We can afford a taxi to follow her, but I doubt she'll go that far. Let's save our money and use our feet for now."

Bailey gave her a long look and nodded. "It'd be difficult to stay out of range in a cab. We can always change our minds if she gets too far away."

Good. At least he wasn't trying to tell her what to do. Sam had to make an effort to walk normally as they strolled down the sidewalk in the same general direction the hired car had gone. She told herself her ankle could use the exercise.

Since Bailey was keeping a constant eye on his watch and they didn't want to look too out of place, she let herself enjoy taking in the sights. The city at night was alive with lights and crackling with energy. All around them.

By the time they'd walked four blocks, though, she was ready to stop and rest. And she could, since Kirin had once more appeared as a blip on the locator and they confirmed her to be inside a nightclub. A fancy, classy-looking place with an attached restaurant.

Sam wished she had seen the woman entering, but there was no arguing with the watch. So they backed off to a safe distance and waited.

Looking up at Bailey's face high above her, Sam needed to say something before the man barged in with advice of his own. "I need to give my ankle a break."

He wisely refrained from comment and simply nodded, then stared across and down the street.

Sam smiled to herself. "She'll take her leisure, dining and dancing, I'm sure. So why don't you get us some dinner?" Those gyros had been hours ago, and they needed to keep up their strength. "I'll wait and watch." She sat down on a short and seemingly pointless concrete post.

Bailey nodded his approval. *It's better than giving me advice.* Then, without a word, he walked off in the other direction, to make sure he didn't show up on Kirin's locator screen. Just on the off chance. It *was* nice to be able to rely on his intelligence, not to make a stupid mistake in something like that.

Apparently Bailey's assessment of how long the woman would linger agreed with Sam's, because he took his time getting their dinner. Even better, the man offered her an explanation as he handed over a pair of loaded hotdogs. Cheese and chili and onion and relish and mustard.

"I wanted to get us something cheap but filling. We'll want to conserve our resources all we can."

Which sentiment Sam agreed with. "Good job, Bailey. And good thinking." And good food.

As she balanced them, one in either hand, she thought about all the restaurants and cafés and the food carts. *Do none of these people ever eat in their own homes? Can they even cook?*

Bailey munched mechanically on his own food. Not knowing how much time they had, she inhaled her own and tried not to think about the luxurious vittles Kirin was doubtless partaking of. Especially since it was all profit from theft and murder. If Sam allowed the thought it would interfere with her own digestion.

She finished her second hotdog and wiped her mouth with a stiff paper napkin Bailey handed over to her. Like a gentleman he disposed of both their trash while she continued to rest her ankle. After he returned, he slumped beside her to keep vigil. She squinted down the street at the entrance to the restaurant, while Bailey's eyes dropped to his watch.

Now was the time for Sam to take the reins.

She started without looking at him. "You know what that woman is—you said so yourself. You've agreed she must be brought to justice and that right now we're the only ones in a position to do anything about that."

"Which doesn't mean we *should* do anything." Bailey kept his eyes on his locator screen. "Nor do I know how we'd do it, if it *were* up to us."

Sam tried to control her irritation. "Kirin can't be allowed to keep that money, to profit from murdering Harold. You know that. More importantly, you understand why she can't be permitted to keep that leader device."

"I know, Sam." Then he shook his head. "But I don't know what's the right thing to do about it. If we have the right to stop her. It's taking the law into our own hands."

She found her jaw clenched tight and had to relax before she could speak again. "We not only have the right, we have a moral duty, because there's no one else. It may go against your training, but I don't have any such inhibition."

Bailey kept shaking his head, but he didn't continue arguing with her.

She took a deep breath. "One way or another, we'll have to do something. I don't yet know what that is, but I will, and I'll expect your help."

She got no response, which was better than the alternative. They both just sat there in silence.

It was past midnight when Sam finally saw the woman leave, at the same time as Bailey grunted at his watch. Kirin must've been having quite the party. The woman had always enjoyed being the center of attention, and having had to lay low for a few days must have taken its toll.

Inside, men must've been dancing attendance on her. But when she emerged into the bright, artificial light shining on the club entrance, she was all alone. All Sam could see was red.

Rubies on Kirin's fingers and blue amethysts in her earlobes, gold and diamond and emerald necklaces all draped around the woman's throat. Kirin sparkled in a gaudy display of stolen wealth.

TB

Sam growled low in her chest. "Why didn't you tell me?"

Bailey must have noticed. The woman had met with some dealer already—it must have been today in her hotel room right under their very noses. Now she was wearing her ill-gotten gains. Flaunting the wealth she'd gotten over poor Harold's dead body.

Sam felt a rage rising from deep in her heart as she stood there staring at the gall of the woman.

The indignation burned so hot inside of her, it seemed her gaze might sear the woman to ashes as she stood on the curb. It didn't, but Kirin must have felt the glare. She suddenly raised her eyes to look into the night, down the street and across into the darkness where Sam stood.

The same shock passed between the two as had that first time—when Sam had seen Kirin standing over Harold's corpse. And as when she'd watched the woman standing on those steps in the park.

Kirin couldn't possibly have made out Sam so far away and in shadow, but the woman must have felt her presence. Sam could see her looking down at her wrist. Bailey was doing the exact same thing —checking his locator screen.

He glanced over at Sam. "When she left, she got that bit closer. We've become blips."

"No. As close as we are, and so far from her, we will only be one blip. You're as good as invisible."

Kirin had discovered she was still being chased, and she'd think she knew by whom. But she didn't know about Bailey, so that advantage remained—if they got the chance to use it.

Sam knew what would happen next, and it did. Kirin ran. She didn't wait for the hired car that had not yet shown but hailed one of the waiting taxis.

Pulling two twenties from her cache as she ran down the street, Sam waved them at the other cabs and went straight for the one that was quickest off the mark to pull toward her. The advantage of surprise was gone.

Now it was a race, and Sam always ran to win.

The taxi popped its door open for her, and she jumped in, handing the forty dollars to the driver as Bailey ducked his tall frame in after her.

"Follow that cab." Sam pointed at the taxi that had just pulled away with Kirin inside. "Whatever you do, don't lose her." Sam fixed her eagle eye on the target, not wanting to lose track of that particular cab among the swarm of taxis in the street.

The driver leaned back and looked at her over his shoulder. "Excuse me, miss, but—"

"That woman is trying to escape justice. Now get moving."

"Then you should call a cop." But as he said it, he pulled away with a screech and started following the other cab.

Sam needed his continued cooperation. "If she gets away, we won't know where to find her, and the authorities won't be able to find her either."

She squinted as she tried to memorize the details of the cab Kirin had taken while she could still make them out—the number and the slightly bent rear bumper were the only distinguishing features Sam could discern, though. Beside her in the back of the taxi, Bailey said nothing, but she trusted that he was keeping an eye on his locator app. It would be needed if she lost sight of the woman's cab.

The distance Kirin had already gained troubled Sam—if they couldn't rely on the woman having to wait the full twenty-four hours, then she might be able to Travel at any time. And she *would* try when she thought she'd gotten far enough away that Sam wouldn't be taken along for the ride.

Sam knew Kirin was intelligent. However safe the woman had imagined herself until now, she had to have realized that she'd brought her pursuer into the past with her. Twice. Kirin was bright enough to reach the same conclusions about the real range of the Travel field as Sam had.

The woman would try to put as much distance as she could between herself and her pursuer, not relying on what her locator screen indicated.

None of them knew how much difference there was between the supposed range of the Travel field and the reality, though. As Kirin created as much of a gap as she could, Sam would have to try to stay as close as she could manage. Unfortunately the woman was already a good fifty meters ahead of them.

Sam spoke to the driver. "Where do you think she might be heading?"

The man shook his head but kept his eyes on the road. "We're moving through the Upper West Side toward Harlem. If she keeps going this way, it will take her into the Bronx. If she's running, could be she's headed for a bridge, to get off the island."

"And how far will that taxi driver be willing to take her?"

The man laughed. "Depends how much she can pay him, I suppose."

Sam knew Kirin had the money to go as far as she wanted, and a lot farther than Sam. She didn't tell the driver how limited their own funds were.

If Kirin had realized she didn't have to outrun Sam but simply outlast her, or more accurately outspend her, they'd be sunk. Even now Kirin might be racing to an airport to lose them entirely.

Though that might be a moot point, the way she had her driver racing along. The distance between the two taxis was steadily increasing.

Sam felt her stomach start to tie in knots as they crossed one of the bridges and followed Kirin's cab onto a broad highway.

Sam handed a wad of bills up to the driver. "Go faster, please. We have to catch up somehow."

The cabbie accelerated. "I'll go as fast as I can, safely. But I won't risk my life trying to keep up with a lunatic."

"I wouldn't want you to." She was willing to risk her own life, and maybe even Bailey's, but she didn't want the death of a bystander on her conscience.

After a few minutes, the driver volunteered another comment. "It looks like they're gonna stay on 95 for a while—does that give you any idea where she might be headed?"

"It might if I knew where this 95 went."

"It'll take them up into Westchester County and then along the coast into Connecticut. I don't know how far you think this bird is gonna fly, buy it'll take a lot more money to go that far."

Sam caught the hint. The man was willing to be helpful, but he wouldn't be taking them any farther than they could pay. She covertly checked her cash reserves. She didn't have much left, but it was all or nothing now, so she handed the last of her hoard up to the driver.

"Tell me when that's running out." She held out her hand to Bailey. His face was grim, but he handed over the money he'd tried to give her earlier that day. "And please try to keep from falling any farther behind."

Sam could still see Kirin's cab ahead in the distance, but the woman had already put more than a hundred meters between them. Either her battery hadn't recharged enough for Travel, or more likely she wanted to gain more ground first—as she was managing to do quite easily.

Fifteen minutes later, Sam estimated that they had fallen a good quarter mile behind the other taxi —or four times the supposed range. However much of a fudge factor there might be, it couldn't be that big. Kirin was too far away.

If the woman Traveled now, she wouldn't take them with her, and Sam could see no way to catch up.

It was then that the driver coughed and glanced back at her with a sheepish smile. "I'm afraid I'm going to need more money soon. Not that I'm saying you're not good for it, but..."

Sam nodded. She wasn't 'good for it'—not for much longer even if she used Bailey's supply. The chase had become futile already, and she refused to compound her failure by defrauding the cabbie.

"You'd better find a place to pull over and let us out then. We can't afford to go much farther."

The driver kept speeding along. "I can't just let you off on the side of the highway. What'll you do?"

"I don't know—but we'll be fine. Please just let us out."

Chapter 9

Sam wanted to cry as the cab began to slow and drift across the lanes toward the shoulder. But she held back the tears as she watched Kirin's taxi speed off toward the horizon. Sam wouldn't allow herself to indulge in self-pity.

She fought against just giving up. She knew the general direction the woman was headed in. Maybe they could guess where she was headed, find a way to get there ahead of her. Before she used her watch to Travel. There was another branch of the bank in Boston—Kirin could be going there.

Sam let her eyes drop to her lap and looked at her clenched fists. *Admit the truth. You've failed.* Kirin would Travel, and then there would be, could be, no more pursuit. It was over.

Then Sam was tumbling and skidding along the ground.

Chapter 10

The Realtor's Tale

July 7th, 2000 Little Piece, NY

ANYA leaned back in her chair, and Mrs. McGlinty shoveled scrambled eggs from the pan and onto the plate. Tate was forking down his fried potatoes fast to try and make room for plenty of eggs. Turner and Nye were munching on cereal and slurping coffee—even though the pair were already stimulated to the point they could barely contain themselves.

"Of course, I don't mind getting up early," said Mrs. McGlinty as she moved down to spoon the rest of the eggs out for Tate. "I mean, I always do myself. My guests don't usually get started so early though. I'm not used to making a big breakfast at this hour." Outside a rooster crowed.

Anya smiled. "Don't worry, Helen. This meal is wonderful. And we wouldn't want you to put yourself out for us anyway." Despite their being paying guests. "It's incredible that you whipped all this up so fast."

Anya wasn't sure whether their hostess had intended to sound apologetic or aggrieved—the truth was, Mrs. McGlinty was fishing. The woman wondered why they were all getting up before dawn and heading out so early. She wouldn't just ask, though.

Anya and Tate were used to rising this early and liked it. Turner and Nye had plenty of practice getting up with the sun, even if they didn't care to, but today they meant to get a quick start back into the city—not that they'd been gone long enough to miss it yet. Anya certainly didn't.

It had taken until midday on Wednesday to finish all their preparations before hiring a car to drive them to Little Piece. Now Nye insisted on turning right around and heading back. The girl wanted to hurry up and document the baseline for the current version of New York City, and Turner had generously volunteered to chaperone her this weekend. *I can count on him to keep her out of trouble.*

By the time the two returned Sunday evening, Anya hoped to have already found the right property and settled everything. Then they'd no longer need to stay at the bed and breakfast.

Mrs. McGlinty was nice, and a great cook, but it was awkward enough trying to keep their business private—living under the roof of an inveterate gossip was taking its toll on Anya's nerves.

She decided to throw the woman a scrap. "The young people are traveling into the city this morning, and there's plenty they want to get done before they come back." Nye had her research, and Turner not only needed to keep an eye on the girl, Anya had him checking on the classified ads they'd placed in several papers, as well as investigating their other options. So he'd have his hands full.

A genteel honk sounded from outside, so Anya quickly added, "And Tate and I are going with Mrs. Grant to take a look at a few properties. I'm afraid I asked her to come at dawn."

Nye remained focused on her coffee, but Turner was paying attention. Tate shoveled his remaining eggs down the hatch and stood. Anya followed his example and pushed back from the table, smiling at Mrs. McGlinty as she rose. "Thank you, again, for a really marvelous breakfast."

"You're welcome, Miss Anya." Their hostess chuckled. "You're not setting up your own bed and breakfast are you? Not that I'd mind—"

"Nothing like that. We're just looking for some kind of summer retreat. For ourselves and some of our colleagues."

Mrs. McGlinty's eyebrows rose. "The work you people do—"

Anya cut in again, "I really don't want to keep Mrs. Grant waiting."

Turner stepped into the breach. "Your place is so nice here, Helen, I'm tempted to stay and forego the trip into the city."

Nye shot Turner a hard glare under her bangs, but Mrs. McGlinty blushed. "Oh, you!"

This afforded Anya the opportunity to grab her bag and scurry out of the dining room without further conversation—she just waved to their hostess and flashed a final fretful glance at Turner and Nye. As Anya strode to the front door and onto the porch, she hoped they'd be moving into a new home today. Tate trundled out after her. At least *he* didn't seem to be anxious about anything.

She worried about the arrangements she'd had to make with the bank, in order for them to be able to purchase some property—and that was in addition to getting the debit card. She'd been assured everything would go smoothly once they found the place they wanted. But she didn't want to rush and pick the wrong one, so she tamped down her eagerness and sense of expectation.

She breezed down the walkway with Tate in tow to the curb, where Mrs. Grant sat in the driver's seat of her station wagon playing with her cell phone. Of course, it wouldn't be play but business. From her limited interaction with the woman, Anya thought the realtor must breathe business like most people breathed air. *TB*

Mrs. Grant nodded at them as they approached the car but kept talking on the phone. Anya opened the back door for Tate and then slid into the passenger seat next to the realtor.

"—and I'll call back as soon as the papers have been signed." Mrs. Grant ended her call and turned to Anya with a practiced smile. "Sorry to keep you waiting, but there's always something."

The woman turned her smile on Tate and then returned to Anya. "I have three potentials to show you today, and they should all satisfy your requirements." The realtor handed Anya a stack of folders. "Take a look while we drive if you want, but I've got the details memorized so I can just rattle them off." Mrs. Grant paused, but when Anya didn't respond, the woman continued, "This first property I'll show you is probably the one. You may not need to even look at the others."

The realtor continued talking while the station wagon glided down the early morning streets. The people in this small rural town were already up and around, but there just weren't that many of them, so it felt quiet and peaceful. Anya would love it here, and so would Tate. It might drive Nye crazy though, staying too long in this isolated spot, which would mean she'd make even more trips into the city.

Anya would have to figure out how to supervise the girl to keep her out of trouble. If Turner didn't want to spend so much time in the city chaperoning Nye, the job would fall to Anya, since Tate was solid but not up to a lot of running around.

She'd recovered three of her fellow Travelers—she needed to find the others, not lose any of those she'd managed to gather so far.

She jerked her head up as the car turned onto a nicely paved driveway. A vast Colonial mansion sat on a slight hill. But she didn't see a barn.

Mrs. Grant glanced her way. "You see how it's sitting up there on the hill. It has a great view of the countryside. And you said you needed a big house."

What Anya saw was an expensive luxury, and one that sat almost in the middle of the town. She'd asked for a place with more acreage, more privacy. And while they had plenty of money to spend, they didn't have it to waste. "What about the barn?"

The realtor looked slightly uncomfortable. "Of course it *has* a barn. I don't know that it's exactly the kind of barn you asked for, but as for the house itself—it's magnificent. You'll see."

"I'm sure it is, Mrs. Grant." Anya smiled. "And since the house is that lovely, let's take a look at the barn first."

Mrs. Grant's smile had returned, but faltered a bit before regaining form. "You're the client." No doubt the seller was a client, too.

Ms. Dervan had explained how things tended to work in the kind of small towns they'd be searching for property in, and so far Little Piece accorded with her description. It made Anya consider how much the realtor might talk. Their group couldn't expect their conduct to go without comment, but it would be better if Mrs. Grant didn't spread the word about their peculiar requests.

The station wagon turned to drive down a worn path around the side of the house. Behind it sat the so-called barn, which was more of a shack. Just by looking at the outside of it, Anya could tell it didn't meet her specifications. They would require a big empty space for Traveling, since even if they stood right next to each other they'd still separate some. And they didn't want to worry about being seen, and that meant indoors—a big empty barn.

Anya started shaking her head as soon as she saw it. "I'm sorry Mrs. Grant, but having a big barn is essential for us. I'm afraid this place simply won't be suitable."

"If you could just take a look inside the house..."

Anya kept shaking her head as she flipped back through the folders. The realtor gave a soft sigh, but she was a practical woman and turned the car back toward the front of the house and drove back down to the main road. While the realtor was focused on that, Anya picked out their new home.

She held the folder up high in front of the windshield, spread open so Mrs. Grant could see. "This place looks like it has a big enough barn."

The realtor sighed and shoved the folder out of her face. That's not the barn, that's the house. But the barn is almost as big. Maybe bigger."

Anya simply nodded. "It sounds just right."

"I have to tell you, it's on low lying land. Sometimes when we get the really heavy rains, it kind of floods. You'd better get flood insurance."

"I'm sure it won't be that bad—the roof doesn't leak, does it?"

Mrs. Grant shook her head. "No, the house and barn are both in good repair, and solid. No problems there. But while the house is large, it's got a lot of rooms. It's built cramped—not a lot of space to move around in."

"But the barn isn't like that, is it?"

"No, the barn is airy. Lots of space and light. I think I'd rather live in that barn than the house—if it wasn't for the lack of bathrooms and a kitchen."

Which allayed Anya's concerns. It sounded the perfect place for their purposes. "We may spend a lot of time working in the barn."

"This work..."

Anya decided she'd better say something. "Art. And crafts—that sort of thing. More recreational than work." Now she'd have to take up painting.

Mrs. Grant nodded. Apparently that was an explanation that made sense. "That should be alright, then. But another thing I have to mention..." The realtor hesitated. "This is quite a ways out of town. I know you wanted privacy, but it's not exactly the, well, best location."

Anya shook her head. "If you're trying to tell me it's not a nice area, Mrs. Grant, I won't believe you. I don't believe there's a bit of Chickadee County that's not nice."

"Well..." The realtor gave a little cough. "Some bits of it are nicer than others."

"As long as we've got a nice quiet place where everyone can get away for the summer and relax in peace, we'll be fine."

The realtor sighed. "You may be happy with the next place at that." And she slowed the station wagon and turned down a wide gravel road between two trees and drove past a long metal gate that had been left wide open.

Anya looked into the distance to get a glimpse of their new home. The large wood house was painted forest green and the roof was bright orange. A vast garden spread around one side of the house, and a gigantic barn behind cast a huge shadow over it.

The more Anya saw of the place, the more she fell in love. She turned to give Mrs. Grant a wide smile. "I love it—the garden, that *roof*."

"It's a metal roof, you know—when it rains it'll make an awful racket."

"Perfect." Anya started daydreaming of listening to the drumbeat of the rain on the metal roof. It reminded her of her childhood. She was sure this would be their new home now.

The realtor coughed. "I suppose you'll want to see the barn first?"

Anya nodded. "We'll want to look at the whole place before we make a decision, but I think this is it. But it's the barn that will settle the question."

Mrs. Grant eased past the side of the house and drove up to the barn. After she stopped the car and they all got out, she broached a new subject. "I don't know what your plans are for transportation—did you plan to drive up here for the summer? In your own vehicles? Or will you be needing to rent something..."

Anya shook her head. Without proper identification, she doubted they'd be able to rent a car, or even buy one. They certainly couldn't drive, legally speaking. "I think we'll just buy a few bicycles for getting around up here."

The realtor goggled but made no comment. Anya wondered if it would be such a hardship to cycle into town and around. Perhaps one of them should research the laws and local ordinances to see what kinds of transportation they could operate without the need for identification.

Anya sighed under her breath. Everywhere she looked there were a lot of these little problems that needed to be taken care of. Many due to the Travelers' lack of proper identification. Someone should have foreseen the issue.

She set aside her worries about those problems and paid attention to the barn in front of them. She glanced at the house and back again. The barn had not been painted—it was simple varnished wood. It did look solid, well built. And as they approached the giant double doors, Anya lifted her eyes to see big windows high up, which would indeed let in lots of light.

Tate walked in front of her and pulled the heavy doors open. He stood aside and waved the ladies in. They stepped into the big empty space smelling of sawdust and mildew, and Anya saw that those high windows ran all along each wall of the barn. They'd be a nightmare to clean.

Then she noticed the wooden staircases on each side of the doorway, against the wall and going up to a narrow loft that ran all the way around the upper level, just under those windows. *So that's how they can be cleaned, on the inside anyway.*

Anya asked Mrs. Grant about how they'd clean the outside of those windows.

The realtor cleared her throat. "That's another thing I wanted to mention—I presume you'll want help with the upkeep, especially if you're only going to be around in summer." Seeing Anya nod, Mrs. Grant continued, "What kind of help will you want? And do you need staff to help in the summer season as well? For cooking and cleaning? What about the lawn and the garden?"

Anya considered. They wouldn't want the contemporaries coming in and out while the Travelers were using the place for research. "We'll take care of everything ourselves during the season. The rest of the year we'll want someone to take care of everything—the lawn and garden especially."

Mrs. Grant nodded. "Old Bill Wheeler lives in the neighborhood, and he's a great gardener—I'm sure he'll be available to take care of the outdoors. What about the house itself? Live-in caretakers?"

Anya shook her head. "I don't think that will be necessary—we won't be leaving anything valuable behind. All we'll need is someone to come by regularly and air the place out, dust and such."

"I can recommend some people who'll keep the house in order for you."

Anya smiled. "Thank you. We'll have the bank pay them directly, so they don't have to contact us."

The realtor nodded again. "But if anything does come up, we'll need some kind of emergency contact information."

Anya sighed. "I'll give you someone you can get hold of at the bank—they can either deal with any situation themselves or contact us." Which would be difficult, since Anya and the others would simply not exist outside of the summer. Traveling through the rest of the year, they'd miss whatever happened in the interim. That couldn't be helped. Returning home would take long enough without living in real time. *Though the slow path does have its appeal.*

She turned around, taking a long look at the interior of the barn and anticipating the time she'd be spending here. Satisfied, she started walking back up to the house.

The realtor called from behind her. "You don't mind if I drive back up? I can park by the door. It'll make it easier when we leave."

Anya called back over her shoulder. "I want the exercise. Tate can ride with you if he'd like."

Tate must've wanted to walk, as he came trudging up to Anya. They both watched Mrs. Grant give a little wave through the car window as she backed up past them and turned the car toward the house.

While they had their moment of privacy, Anya spoke to her helper. "The barn is perfect for Traveling. If it doesn't collapse while we're gone."

Tate smiled. "You worry too much, Leader. It's solid. And even if it got knocked down by a tornado or something, we'd just land on top of the rubble—since we can only come through in empty space. We likely wouldn't be seen out here."

"Yes, I know I worry too much. Right now I'm anxious about Turner and Nye—did they get to the city alright? Who knows what trouble Nye could be in already?"

"You're a mother hen." At least he said it with his smile intact.

They were already coming up to the house, and Mrs. Grant, who must've gone in the front, opened the door that led onto the back porch for them and motioned them inside. The woman watched them climb the few short wooden steps.

She must've seen Anya checking her watch. "I know—it's half past six in the morning. Time flies when you're looking at houses."

Anya shook herself to get rid of the worries she had about Turner and Nye—the pair wouldn't even have arrived in the city yet. She needed to focus on her own business.

Following the realtor in off the porch, Anya noticed it led into a utility room, a very narrow space that ran the entire length of the back of the house. There was a washer and dryer, but not much room to use them. *Cramped, indeed.*

Mrs. Grant preceded Anya and the taciturn Tate down a narrow hallway past a number of doors and into a large kitchen. It, too, was cramped, with its big island and the table and chairs and the counter and cabinets jutting out everywhere.

The realtor pointed. "You'll find a long, narrow pantry through one of those doors."

She walked through an open door into another short hallway and led them past a narrow staircase. She ushered them into a large living room stuffed with furniture. A big bay window with a seat looked out onto the front porch. Anya was entranced. *It just keeps getting better.* T&

Mrs. Grant waved her arms around. "There are two ground floor bedrooms around that corner and upstairs a couple more and a master suite with a full bath. There's another one and a half baths up there, and three half baths down here. You might miss the attic under the roof which is hard to find, but it'll get really hot in the summer, so I don't know that you'll want to use it for anything."

Anya nodded and strolled out the other door to find herself in a main hall staring at a second staircase. The steps were quite deep, and it was barely wide enough for her to climb without turning sideways. Tate and Mrs. Grant followed her.

The realtor must've known what she was thinking. "The other stairs aren't quite so narrow."

Anya shook her head. Harold wouldn't want to climb this, so she'd reserve one of the ground floor bedrooms for him. The other would've been for the professor, if he were still with them.

She looked up the staircase for a long moment, fighting back the tears so she could face Mrs. Grant. "I don't think I need to look any more. This is it."

"You can't really go wrong, investing in real estate. Prices always go up. But you should check the place out thoroughly, pay for a professional inspection before you commit yourself."

Anya remembered the price from the folder the woman had given her. Amazing that a home should be so expensive.

She turned to Tate. "Why don't you look around up there and make sure there are no problems? I'll stay down here and take care of business."

Tate nodded without a word and squeezed past Anya to start climbing the stairs. The realtor took a glance back in the living room and then suggested, "Why don't we sit down in the kitchen to go over the paperwork?"

So Anya followed her back, and they both sat at the large circular oak table that took up the space not occupied by the island. Mrs. Grant took a thick folder out of her bag. "Now then, there are a lot of forms to fill out, and I'll have to call the lawyer, Mr. Pistlethorn, to see when we can close."

Anya shook her head. "It won't be that compli-cated." She reached into her own bag and retrieved a folder. The hard work had been done—this part should be easy. "We've already made our arrange-ments with Mr. Pistlethorn." The local lawyer with the unfortunate name seemed to handle all the real estate transactions in town.

She continued, "The trustees at our bank have prepared the funding, and the trust itself will be the official owner, the purchaser of the property. It's all been taken care of." She slid out a sheet of paper. "I simply sign this authorization, confirming the spe-cific property and the agreed price and fees. Then you can drop it off with Mr. Pistlethorn. The bank-ers and the lawyers will handle the rest. While you and I get on with life."

Mrs. Grant gaped for a moment, then smiled a genuine smile. "This is a pleasant surprise."

The realtor handed Anya a financial disclosure sheet with the full purchase price with closing and other costs detailed, then watched as Anya copied the information onto her authorization form. She signed her name at the bottom and then pulled the ink pad she'd bought from her bag and affixed her thumbprint next to her signature. She slid the com-pleted form over to Mrs. Grant with a smile.

"There now." Anya dropped the ink pad back into her bag. "All done. What next?"

The realtor returned to her usual businesswoman persona. "Since no one is in residence and only the formalities remain, why don't I give you the keys now? So you can start making this place over. I can tell you're eager to get started."

Anya grinned. "That sounds great. But could you give us a ride back into town? We need to buy some supplies—sheets and dishes and groceries. I suppose we'll have to take care of getting the power turned on first, for the refrigerator. And of course we'll need a couple of bicycles and maybe a wagon. Does someplace in town sell wagons? Or bicycles for that matter?"

Mrs. Grant was shaking her head—not in negation but in wonder. "Of course. I'll take you there. And I can show you where the electric company is. Sounds like you're going to have a busy day."

Anya didn't mind that. They'd also need to get their things from Mrs. McGlinty's—no need to stay there another night. They had their new home now, and Anya couldn't wait to move in.

Chapter 11

No Way Out

November 30th, 1997 Midtown Manhattan

MATT still held the black leather bag in his arms and stood on the same sidewalk in front of the same stores, but the thugs were gone—and so was Page. He looked around wildly and had to force himself to breathe slow. In just a minute he had calmed down and could think straight and began to scan his surroundings in every direction.

He knew people got separated when they Traveled together. Not only had Page told him, but he'd experienced the phenomenon himself. If she'd been pulled out of his arms that time but lost her helpers completely when she had arrived in two thousand, then the difference in dislocation had to be either a function of the amount of time spanned or the relative physical distances involved.

Matt checked his watch. They'd Traveled exactly one year into the past. Since the separation when they'd gone back two and a half had been minimal, Page would be right here if it were the first, so it had to be the latter. Meaning she shouldn't be far away, since she had been close enough to touch. Now the question was how to find her.

Before he could even try to answer that, his eye was caught by her brilliant red head bobbing up the street toward him. *Of course.* He should've known that Page could and would track him down. *I've got the money.*

He stood still and watched through the gaps in the crowds as she approached, wanting to see her face. When she appeared though, she was staring at her watch, and all Matt could see was the top of her head—then when she raised her eyes and saw him, she was glaring.

Matt grinned back. He wondered what her first words would be—he couldn't begin to guess.

"Was that really necessary?" She frowned, then leaned forward to peer into the top of the bag.

"Completely. Start thinking of New York City as a jungle. If you don't want to get in more trouble."

"This *jungle* has some great shopping. I saw a store just down the street—and now we can go."

Matt gaped. "You want to go shopping? Right now?" He looped his hand through the straps of the bag and folded the top closed in a fist. Page had said she'd be getting a new one anyway. He grabbed her elbow with his other hand and propelled her out of the flow of foot traffic.

She stared at him for a long moment. "My device shouldn't have recharged sufficiently to Travel. Clearly it had, but it couldn't have had a full charge. So we should wait the full twenty-four hours before we try to Travel again. I can spend that time shopping. I still need better clothes, don't I?"

He looked her up and down and shook his head. "You said it feeds off my body's own electrical field —well, light bulbs tend to blow if I get too close. So we may not have to wait quite that long before we can Travel."

"It's a Sunday. Even if we *could* Travel sooner, we might as well wait. The bank won't be open until tomorrow morning, and after I've been shopping I may need to get more cash."

"I suppose you used that GPS thing you mentioned two and a half years in the future. To find me so fast."

Page nodded. "Of course. What else would you expect me to do?"

"But I didn't know how to look for you. How do you use that tracking function?"

She shook her head. "I thought you understood I wasn't going to show you how to use my device."

Matt grinned. "Because of our trust issues. You said you wouldn't show me how to Travel. Which I managed anyway. And you want me sticking close, don't you?"

Page glared at him for a while before nodding. "It's so simple you shouldn't need me to show you, but I guess it will be quicker this way."

Holding out her own watch so he could see how she operated it, Page pressed the bottom left button.

"I only press once on this device, but press the same button twice on mine to get to the locator app. That blip in the center of the screen is you—it would be me appearing on my watch. If I'm out of range, a red bar on an edge of the screen shows the compass direction in which you can find me."

"Simple indeed." Though it would make more sense if the red bars indicated the relative direction rather than compass points. "So how did we end up in the same place we left from this time? Instead of being thrown clear to Long Island?"

"It must be because we each had a device when we Traveled this time. I told you one device wasn't meant to carry two people. It threw things off."

"So this time, everything worked right."

"No. At least, the spatial displacement on landing isn't supposed to happen."

Matt winked at her. "Sounds like someone got their sums wrong. A mathematician. Couldn't have been you by any chance?" eye roll* ict

Page glared. "No, not my area. Now, if you're finished asking questions, why don't we get on with some shopping?"

"Why don't we find someplace to eat first? I haven't eaten since—" *Breakfast in the summer of two thousand.* "I don't know when you last ate."

She shrugged. "We ate before we left. But I *am* starting to feel hungry, so find us a place. At least four stars."

"I don't think so." He would have to put up with enough of that sort of environment at the places she liked to shop. "I want to eat now instead of spending an hour waiting for a table before I even get to see a menu."

Matt was definitely getting hungry—chasing after Page was giving him an appetite. He pointed. "See the hotdog stand across the street. That's fast."

"That's a long way from the kind of meal I was thinking of."

"It's also quicker, easier, and delicious. And the sooner we eat, the sooner you can shop." And he'd need a full stomach to endure that experience.

"That makes sense." Without hesitating, she'd already started striding down the sidewalk, making for the intersection and expecting him to catch up.

TB ict

But when they reached the cart, Page shook her head as she peered at the piled-high hotdogs others were walking away with. "Too messy. Is there anything fast and neat?"

Matt sighed. "Maybe a burrito—they're all over the place and less messy than anything else I know. At least that we could find in a hurry."

They still had to wander down several blocks to find a burrito vendor, but Page enjoyed examining the stores they passed. When they lined up before the cart, Matt realized he'd better not dip into the bag for cash. This meal would be on him. At least he had enough money left for that.

His free hand dug out his wallet and handed it over to Page. "While I'm carrying your bag, this is too awkward for me to manipulate. Keep it for now and pay for our meal."

When they reached the head of the line, he ordered two of the giant wraps. Page gave the vendor a twenty and told him to keep the change. *She'll pay me back for that.*

Matt wondered how much of the burrito she'd manage to eat as they walked toward Times Square. She focused on each and every shop they passed and still scarfed down her food. Without paying *it* any attention. When she finished, she absentmindedly tossed the wrapper in a nearby waste can. Then she wanted to go into a store.

Hampered as he was by having only one hand to eat with, Matt *hadn't* finished however. Swallowing a big bite of burrito, he protested. "There are better shops further on."

Page shook her head but kept walking. "With all these restaurants everywhere—doesn't anyone ever eat at home?"

He thought that was rich coming from a woman who didn't seem the type to do any cooking herself. Then he realized her question gave him an opportunity.

He shoved the last remnant of his meal into his mouth and waited until it cleared his throat. "That's a complicated subject. I'm willing to expound on it for you. In exchange, you could tell me some things about the future. I admit I'm curious."

"The question was rhetorical. And if I need to find out more about contemporary dining habits, I will do *proper* research. Not rely on the unsupported anecdotes of a biased contemporary subject."

"I see." And he did. He agreed with her reasoning, in terms of methodology, even as he missed the chance to satisfy his own curiosity. Well, Page was loose enough with the little details—he only had to get her to talk more and he ought to be able to pick up a picture of the future world she came from.

Noticing that he'd finished his burrito, she held up a hand to stop him. Then she looked around at the shops around them and picked one. She waved at the main entrance to a building full of expensive boutiques. "I want to shop in there."

Matt sighed and tossed his empty wrapper in a trash can. "I'm not stopping you. I'm just following your lead, remember?" He wasn't about to suggest where she should buy her clothes. Considering her attitude, he didn't hold out hope she'd ask his opinion what clothes she looked good in either.

Page squinted at him for a moment before pulling the large glass door open. Grinning, he stepped through ahead of her. Now that he had both hands free, he shifted the heavy bag full of money back up into his arms.

He stopped and let Page precede him. Presumably she knew where she'd want to shop, but as soon as they had entered, it occurred to him how out of place they looked among the well-heeled clientele. Hopefully people would assume Page was eccentric —a star or something. She looked the part. Matt surely had to look as if he were waiting attendance on her. *I've turned into a gofer.*

She wandered first into a jewelry store and took half an hour to examine earrings, finger rings, and necklaces—while Matt stood there and tried not to sweat. A security guard stared at them suspiciously the entire time. And after all that, Page didn't want to buy anything.

Matt goggled when she told him. "Why not? I don't care about jewelry, but it seemed nice."

"I don't care much about jewelry myself. I just wanted to look at what they had."

Matt sighed. The burrito had left his throat dry, and he needed water, but this place didn't have any conveniently located water fountains that he could see. Or bathrooms. There had to be facilities somewhere, but he didn't want to have to search through the building for them.

Besides, he couldn't leave Page alone. Although right now she needed him to carry her cash around, he wanted to stick close so he'd be there if and when she got into trouble. Which seemed only a matter of time. Thinking of that, he checked and saw that the afternoon was already passing—this late in the year it would be growing dark soon.

She proceeded to spend over an hour browsing through three more shops, examining all manner of hats, scarves, belts, and bracelets. She hadn't even started on shoes yet, much less actual clothes. Only the accessories. It was going to be a very long day— maybe a long night at this rate.

Then she pushed into a purse store.

Matt tried talking to her in a low voice, to avoid attracting attention. "Why here? I'd have thought you'd want to get shoes first, then get your new bag to match them, or your clothes."

Page turned to roll her eyes at him. "Once I find the right purse, I'll look for the shoes to match."

"What about a dress?"

"To wear *where*? First, I'll find something fashionable to wear shopping, then I can concentrate on the luxuries."

Matt couldn't stop the escaping sigh. This was not the Page who had intrigued him when they first met, but it was too late now. Perhaps the other Page would return once this one had finished shopping.

A thin man with a ghost of a beard and a plastic smile walked up to them with a questioning look in his eyes. "Can I help you find anything?"

Matt shook his head, and Page just stared at the man, who shifted his gaze to the bag Matt was holding. "Not many places carry that brand, but we sell that purse here." The man stretched to try and peer inside the bag. "It looks brand new. Where did you buy it?"

Matt saw the man's eyes were disapproving. Of course it was rude to purchase something at a competitor's and then waltz in here flaunting it, though he doubted that concerned Page. "Not here. We did *not* know you carried it."

Page gave the man a haughty stare. "It *is* brand new, but I didn't buy it. I'm not sure where it came from." She turned her glare on Matt. "It *could* have been bought at this very store."

The man cocked his head at her. "You admit it's brand new, but you say you didn't *purchase* it?" His welcoming smile had faltered.

Page started shaking her head, and Matt knew she was giving the man the wrong idea. *But he can't think Page shoplifted the bag, not from here.* Then he glanced around and saw the security guard from the jewelry store hanging out at the entrance to this shop. He'd left his post and followed them through the mall. *Why?*

Matt hurried into the breach. "A friend bought this for her. The woman didn't say where."

Page nodded. "The receipt's still in the bag."

Right away Matt realized it was a mistake. He tried and failed to catch her eye to give her a meaningful look. "Why don't you show it to him?"

Page looked at him now, clearly realizing she'd landed them in it. She sighed and reached into the bag. Matt could feel the tension rising in the atmosphere. She grabbed the papers from on top of the cash and looked at them before handing one over— hopefully it wasn't the bank receipt for this money Matt was holding.

The man examined the receipt she'd given him, and his weak smile turned to consternation. "It's a rather stupid forgery. They carry that purse as well, but who knows if they'll still be selling it a year from now? No one *bought* this, did they?"

The little man waved to a tall man in a tan suit who was emerging from a back room. The newcomer was slim and athletic, and Matt recognized him as store security and also noticed that the guard by the door had gone on alert, his hand hovering over his holstered weapon.

Tan security man approached them slowly. "I'm afraid I'll need to see what else you have in that bag. I'm sure you understand." He held out his hand.

Matt didn't understand that one bit, but he had to buy time while he calculated all the variables. "I have to decline. *I'm* afraid this bag and its contents are the property of the lady, and I won't be handing them over to a stranger."

Once they got a look at all that cash and a bank receipt also dated a year in the future, there would be no explanation that would satisfy the cops. And Matt presumed the police had already been called, were on their way right now. He couldn't delay any further. He'd have to cooperate.

Tan security man reached into his jacket pocket and withdrew his identification and detective's license to show them. "I'm in charge of security here, and I'm afraid I must insist."

Matt glanced at it but didn't really pay it any attention. "Of course, we *want* to help." He looked at Page. "If you'll just hand me that other receipt, I'm sure it will help the gentleman understand."

Her eyes held confusion, but Page passed over the paper without question, into one of Matt's waiting hands stretching out from underneath the bag. He folded the paper roughly in one hand while his other grabbed her wrist.

He looked back at tan security man. "Take the receipt and the bag and the time you need to satisfy yourself."

The detective nodded and replaced his identification in his suit pocket before reaching out to take the paper and the purse. Matt shifted, and the bag toppled forward into the other man's arms.

"I'm so sorry." Matt grabbed at the receipt and the bag and helped the heavy weight push the man backward.

Fortunately Page reached out to take the paper out of Matt's hand and stuffed it into the top of the purse. Matt stepped forward and slid his hand under the man's elbow and lifted to help him loose his balance backward as Page helped take the weight of the bag off his hands. Tan security man tumbled to the ground.

Page kept firm hold of the purse, and Matt kept his grip on Page's wrist and dragged her toward the back of the store and the other door. The one that detective had come from. Which was preferable to going through the security guard—who was probably drawing his weapon even now.

Matt didn't turn to look, just pulled Page along with him. The guard wouldn't fire on an unarmed woman, especially not in the back as she fled. The man yelled 'Stop!' while Matt dragged her into the back room. He hoped she was still holding tight to all that money—not because he cared, but because he could imagine how cranky Page would be if it got lost. And he knew she would blame him.

He didn't pause to examine the room—he just scanned swiftly, noting a small space crowded with extra stock and a desk with phone, and a door opening out into a white corridor. He ran toward it and thankfully Page kept up. He pulled her through into the hallway and closed the door behind them. But he had no way to bar it shut.

Then she wrested her hand away from his grip and lifted the heavy bag she still carried up into her arms. "What now, Matt?"

Busy looking up and down the corridor and trying to think, he didn't have the time to answer her. He saw no hint at an exit to the outside. Their time was running out to escape the building, with those security men surely knowing where they must have run and the police likely on the way. *Of course.*

Not being a seasoned Traveler, he hadn't realized soon enough that they already had the perfect means of escape. *If only they've recharged enough.* They just needed a bit of privacy. And time.

It might not work, but they were running short of options. Matt glanced again at the line of closed doors up and down the hallway, discounting doors with plates proclaiming store names. A door with a staircase sign tempted him briefly. But if it came to a chase through the building, eventually they'd be caught.

It was an unmarked door he looked for, supply closet or restroom or something like that, and one that locked from the inside to buy them time. That should get them a few minutes at least. He hoped. He chose the one closest to them to try first.

The closest unmarked room was already locked though. He ran down to the next possibility. This door opened, and he saw it could be locked.

He shoved Page in ahead of him as he glanced up and down the corridor. No one had yet followed them this far. He ducked into the room after her, swinging the door shut behind him.

He pushed the lock in and prayed. The security people would have to find where he and Page were hiding, then maybe have to find the right key to get at them. If only they didn't discover where he and Page were hiding too quickly.

Worried she wouldn't keep quiet long, he cut in ahead of an anticipated complaint with a whisper. "Stay silent."

"What do you think you're doing?"

At least she'd whispered too. Matt should have known she wouldn't keep quiet at his command.

He lowered his voice even more. "Be quiet. We don't want them to hear us."

Her return whisper was low and harsh. "They'll find us soon enough anyway, won't they?"

Matt glanced around. It was dark in the small room, and he couldn't make out much, but he could feel the cramped space and shelves, and it smelled like a supply closet. "Hopefully we can Travel out of here before they do. That's what I'm counting on."

"Matt, you're a gambler." Page turned to look at him in the dark. "I told you we'd have to wait a full day for my device to recharge. I know we Traveled early before, but that's why we'll have to wait longer this time. And it's only been a few hours."

He was glad she couldn't see the consternation on his face. It had felt a lot longer than that. "And *I* told *you* light bulbs blow if I get too close. Maybe it'll have enough of a charge—if it can even take us one day into the future or past, we'll be free." Anyway, he wasn't going to just give up.

There had to be a way. He grabbed Page by the arms and pulled her close, moving his lips to her ear so she could hear the faintest whisper. "The helper devices like the one you're wearing generate a field of their own? That's what you said. So they have to have a power source. Some kind of battery?"

Page whispered back. "Yes, but they're not programmed to actually generate the field except when linking to a leader. I hope you're not suggesting we try to reprogram it here and now?"

"Does its battery have the same amount of power as yours, though? How much of its charge does it use for just tagging along? If it uses less, it may be fully recharged by now."

He heard her sharp intake of breath. "Matt, we could swap the batteries. It might work."

She was quick, and he appreciated that. He did some fast thinking himself. "When you were holding onto me that first time, this device transported both of us. What would happen if we Traveled that close with both devices? Would they still generate two fields? Would they merge? Multiply?"

She stared at him for a moment, then he felt her hair swish against his face as she shook her head. "I guess we'll find out. It's our best shot. But I'll need light to swap the batteries."

"There must be a light switch here somewhere, but once we turn it on, they may notice through the crack under the door. So we won't have much time to work. Think through exactly what you'll have to do, so you'll be ready once I switch on the light."

"I'm sure I won't have any trouble with that, but things will be iffy enough without you trying to operate my device. You'll have to let me."

Matt nodded in the dark. "Anything we can do to increase the odds. Just leave it on my wrist when we Travel." She could operate it a lot faster anyway. It wasn't like she could take her device back and run at this point.

While they'd been talking, he had stretched out his hand and carefully felt along the wall. "I found the switch. I can turn on the light whenever you're ready."

Page turned to face the door and backed closer into him. "Put your arms around me. We must be as physically close as possible when we Travel, if we want this to have any chance of success. It will help me swap the batteries *and* make it easier to set the coordinates."

She certainly had a lot of reasons he should be holding her—but none of them the right one. Then he heard voices in the corridor and the squeaking of shoes on the waxed floor.

Matt whispered softly. "I don't think we have a lot of time left." He wrapped his arms tight around her, glad she couldn't see him blush.

"Grab the purse straps. I can't hold this bag and do the watches at the same time."

He hardly thought the money was important at this point, but she was clearly determined to take it with them. Hopefully it wouldn't decrease the odds of their actually Traveling.

He didn't want to argue, though, so he snaked his right hand through the straps and wrapped his arm around them and pressed it back against Page. They couldn't be any closer than this. Matt held his left arm up so she could do what she needed to do with the device.

He took a deep breath. "Alright. I'm ready."

"Let me take both of the watches and have them turned over, ready to remove the batteries, before you turn on the light."

He paused to take another deep breath, trying to ignore the sound of the searchers in the hall. "Let me know when and I'll hit the switch."

"I'll try and get us back to your time, Matt, so this can all be over for you."

Page didn't waste any time slipping the watch off his wrist. She removed her own, flipping them over fast. She rested her arms on his as she looked at the devices in each hand. "Go."

He reached out a hand to flip the light switch, immediately returning it to hold her tight, and her purse. He watched her quickly snap the back covers off and swap the batteries. She strapped both their watches back on.

He was watching the crack under the door as he heard the cry from the hallway outside. "I see light under the door of the supply closet. I think they're in here."

Matt closed his eyes and rested his cheek on the top of her head, enjoying the scent of her hair. One way or another, it'd be over soon. Too soon.

He felt her hands moving against his as she fiddled with the watch. He heard her heart beating. Racing.

He heard the door knob rattle, too, and wished she could finish already. Hoped it would work.

"They've locked themselves in. Somebody get the key."

Matt kept his eyes shut and focused on listening to the beating of their two hearts. Two rapid beats falling into synch with each other. In allegro.

Page became his entire world—the feel of her in his arms, the scent of her in his head, and that loud drumbeat in his ears. He could even feel the rest of the world shift around them and disappear.

Leaving only Page.

Chapter 12

The Blood-Stained Pavement

July 3rd, 1991 Little Piece, NY

SAM stood on the grass in the median of the divided interstate as she viewed the left-over bloodstains on the shoulder. She failed to find any other remnants of the accident. Standing behind her, Bailey kept his hand on *her* shoulder, probably so he could pull her to safety should any of the fast moving traffic veer in their direction.

Their own experience had been bad enough, but it could have been much worse. She could imagine only too easily what must've happened *here*—and was grateful that the physical separation had landed them somewhere else. She also thanked God *their* taxi had been slowing when Kirin had Traveled.

TB

Sam and Bailey had found themselves tumbling across a vinyl floor inside a cheap club in the Bronx. Usually, people failed to notice Travelers arriving—they'd unconsciously assume someone had already existed there the previous moment and they simply hadn't noticed. This time though, their landing had created quite a commotion. Thankfully Bailey was big and strong and knew from his days in enforcement how to cow a crowd.

Once they'd extricated themselves they'd had a short talk. Both of them had realized how Traveling out of the moving cab must have affected how they came through. The kinetic energy they couldn't feel inside the taxi had transferred with them and sent their bodies flying just as if the taxi had suddenly braked—only without the inside of the cab to crash into. It didn't require much imagination to know how it must've been for Kirin.

The person generating the main Travel field always arrived in the same physical location they had left from, which meant Kirin would have landed at speed in the middle of a busy highway.

Sam looked away from the bloodstains. "I bet no one considered what would happen if you Traveled from inside a moving vehicle. Or if they did, they failed to mention what it would be like."

"Kirin never thought it through either. She was in too much of a rush to get away."

"Are you saying it's my fault?" Sam believed it was in a way. Her relentless pursuit of Kirin had led to this result.

"No, that's not what I'm saying." Bailey shook his head. "It's hard to believe she really survived."

Sam didn't have any difficulty believing it—she simply accepted the reality. *But what do I do now?*

Unless and until Sam could come up with a way to stop her, the woman would continue doing horrible things. Once she recovered, she'd return to her perfidy. *Wouldn't she?*

Sam couldn't allow that. And it was still only a matter of time before Kirin Traveled away from her pursuers once and for all. Given half a chance.

Sam wondered if Harold would consider what had happened sufficient repayment for the loss of his life—even though she knew things didn't work like that. She needed to go to the hospital.

She'd been grateful to have even an idea where to start searching for Kirin. Back in the Bronx they had found their locator apps pointing to each other rather than the leader device Kirin wore. Bailey had guessed it was because of the distance involved but had said it was something that hadn't been covered in orientation. Another thing.

Sam hadn't paid much attention herself, figuring Harold would tell her what she needed to know. A fine joke that was. But Bailey had conscientiously listened to it all and understood enough of the basic principles to surmise that there was a limit on how far the watches would detect each other. Or at least a limit to what information they'd display.

Anyway, they'd been too banged up and tired to spend much time theorizing, and only had enough money left for several hours rest at a cheap motel, but not enough for another taxi ride far out into the suburbs. The following day, they'd visited a public library to figure out exactly where they'd been when Kirin had Traveled. They'd also checked the newspapers for information about an accident, but there had been nothing.

Last night they'd slept in a stairwell, in a building with poor security, so that they could afford to pay for a bus ticket out to Chickadee County, where they'd Traveled from, their starting point to find out what had happened to Kirin. This morning the bus had dropped them just outside a diner.

Kirin's fate might not have made the news, but the people at the diner were full of the story. After all, it wasn't every day that a beautiful woman wearing an evening gown and a load of jewelry tumbled across the interstate. That Kirin hadn't been hit by some speeding vehicle and killed they considered a mercy. Sam wasn't so sure. Anyway, she and Bailey had heard the details, including the hospital Kirin was at, while devouring their breakfast.

Sam had insisted on first visiting this scene of the accident. She *needed* to see it, and she didn't know yet what she'd do at the hospital. Keeping her hand on Bailey's arm as they walked off the freeway, she wondered how Kirin was reacting to what had happened. *Did it change her?*

The hospital was a fair walk from here, but Sam didn't mind. Her ankle was strong again, despite all the rough treatment and the relative lack of real rest or proper meals. She could do what was needed.

She squinted into the distance. "I believe I can convince them I'm her sister. Since it hasn't been in the papers yet, how else would I know? It should be enough to get me in to see her at least."

Bailey kept his eyes moving in every direction. "I don't know. I think they tended to be fairly strict about hospital visitors."

She bared her teeth at the man. "Don't I look like her sister?"

Bailey looked at her long and hard. "There is a resemblance. There's also your size."

"My size?" She wasn't sensitive about her short stature, but it wasn't like Kirin was a giant.

"It's an advantage. You look like a lost waif. It gives you credibility. Just don't bare your teeth and squint your eyes like that. Give them a weak, trembling smile and open your eyes wide and be a little breathless, and they'll likely let you see her."

Sam tried not to squint. "I suppose you picked up on this kind of thing in enforcement."

Bailey sighed. "Doing what I did, you learn the hard way that you can't always go by appearances. That shy, vulnerable slip of a girl that looks like she wouldn't hurt a fly might slip a knife in you as soon as breathe."

She nodded. Kirin wasn't shy or vulnerable, but you couldn't tell what she was on the inside just by looking. She could seem warm and kind, but butter wouldn't melt in her mouth.

Bailey returned to the present. "Since the truth about the wealth she was wearing doesn't appear to have circulated, scammers probably haven't shown up. So they may not be extra vigilant. Yet."

"So if we get there quick enough, we've got our chance. Why didn't you say so sooner?" She had to get in to see Kirin, one way or another.

"If what they said about the shape she's in has any truth to it, she won't be leaving the hospital any time soon. And it's not like she could imagine that we came through with her. Not at that distance."

That brought up an interesting topic. Sam increased her pace and hoped he could keep up with her and talk at the same time. He might not know how to breathe like her. She suddenly realized how little she really knew about her new partner. It was time to find out more.

"I've got good eyesight." Sam knew that was an understatement, but she tried to be modest. "And I know distances. We were at least a quarter of a mile behind Kirin—and that was before the taxi started slowing down to let us out. I don't care how much of a fudge factor might've been included. There's no way we should have Traveled."

Bailey shook his head slowly. "Obviously there was a way. It happened. We just don't know what it was." He was keeping up with her *and* talking. That was a good sign. "But a quarter of a mile would put us at about four times the purported range. I agree something else must be going on, and we should try to figure it out—it might be useful if we knew. But I paid attention in orientation, and I've no clue what in the world might account for such an effect."

Sam smiled. He'd done the math easily in his head and recognized the crux of the problem right away. That must've been part of his training. She wondered if his pessimism also came from his former career. She wasn't a scientist or engineer, but she felt sure they could solve the problem. Maybe she'd even come up with the answer before him.

She started power walking to push her partner, then set her mind on the mystery of the expanding Travel field. Kirin wouldn't have made a mistake. The woman would have learned what she needed if she'd had to worm it out of Harold.

If Kirin hadn't messed up the operation of the Travel device, there must have been some unknown factor at work. Sam let that question rattle around in her brain and focused on increasing her pace to a light jog. She paid close attention to how her ankle was feeling. *What's the unknown factor?*

After a bit, she felt more confident and would've started to run except she didn't want to leave Bailey behind. He was too big and blocky to run with her. *Or is he?* Surely he'd been made to run in enforcement, and he seemed in good enough shape.

Sam glanced over at her partner. "I don't suppose you're up to running?"

Bailey gave her a rueful grin. "I couldn't run to catch you, I'm sure—but I can manage more than a jog. If you're sure about your ankle?"

For an answer, Sam broke into a run. *Let's see how he does when he's chasing me.*

She didn't look back. She was enjoying the feel of the wind rushing past her too much to see how he was doing—her feet pounding against the ground, and the sweat. It was glorious to run again. So she ran.

Focused on getting to the hospital in good time, she didn't know how long she'd been running when the answer popped into her head. She didn't understand it, but she knew it was right. Perhaps Bailey could explain it to her.

Sam glanced back and saw he was thirty yards behind her. Not bad, but of course she hadn't been going full steam herself, since she had her ankle to consider—and Bailey. She'd have to ask him about the answer later. Right now dealing with Kirin was more important than anything else.

Looking ahead, Sam could see the hospital now looming up over the other buildings before it. Easing her pace so her partner could start to catch up, she thought it looked just like the old pictures. *Why so big? Can there really be so many sick people to need such huge hospitals?* Maybe it explained why so many had died.

By the time they reached the main entrance, her partner had caught up but he was seriously winded. She had slowed gradually and wasn't even a bit out of breath—she would have to fake it if she were to follow her partner's advice.

She stopped in the courtyard and immediately began stretching. Her partner needed to exercise more—he just gasped to a halt and leaned over and put his hands on his knees.

Sam watched him for a minute. "You need to do some cool down stretches. And rest for a bit. You can settle yourself on one of those benches while I go in and see Kirin."

Bailey stood up and shook his head. "I should stick with you."

Sam stared. "It'll be easier for them to believe me if I'm on my own. And though Kirin knew *I* was pursuing her, she shouldn't know about you, hopefully. If she doesn't, we want to keep that advantage if at all possible."

Bailey frowned. He seemed at a loss for what to say. "What if you need my help?"

"Surely you don't think I'll be in danger." The thought popped into her head that he might have a different concern. "Or do you think she's in danger from me? Are you worried about what I might intend, or what I might do without thinking?" Sam went ahead before he could respond, "You just stay here while I go do what I have to do."

He looked her in the eye for a minute, then nodded before turning and walking over to one of the wooden benches. Her partner resisted her leadership less all the time. She hoped he'd know when *not* to obey her.

Turning her gaze away, she ran her mind over the advice he'd given her. She tried to get into the right frame of mind—she would be frantic to find out about her sister, what condition she was in. She took a deep breath and ran into the hospital, darting into the lobby and looking around wildly.

She grabbed the first official-looking person to come within reach. "Help me. I'm looking for my sister. I think she may've been in an accident."

The woman in pink scrubs frowned but put her hand on Sam's arm. "Calm down, now. It'll be fine. Let's go see." And she steered Sam through a pair of large swinging doors back into a little office area with a window out onto the lobby.

Sam thought she should talk more. "I'm just so worried. She was supposed to stop by so we could have dinner last night, but she never showed and I wasn't able to get in touch, and no one seemed to know where she might be and then this morning at the diner I heard about someone who sounds just like my sister being in an accident and having been brought here. Is it her? Is she alright?"

The woman in pink scrubs and a larger woman in a flowery dress who sat on a swivel chair in the little office shared a long look.

The office lady then turned her piercing gaze on Sam. "What's your sister's name?"

"Kirin. Does that mean it *is* her? She was well enough to tell you her name? From what I heard it sounded so bad. I dreaded to think how horrible a shape she'd be in—that she couldn't tell you who she was and she never carries ID on her."

The woman in pink scrubs nodded, but flowery lady didn't look convinced. "Do *you* have ID? Anything to prove you're her sister?"

Sam took a big gulp of air. Her effort to talk fast had made her short of breath in truth. "Oh my gosh.

I rushed over here so fast I forgot to go get my ID—what will Kirin say? I'm always ragging her about that kind of thing and here I am. I'd just gone to the diner for breakfast. Of course I hadn't bothered to take my purse and look at me. I was just so anxious that I ran over without going home even—it would have been quicker to get the car and drive over anyway, but here I am in such a state, I'd probably have forgotten my ID even if I *had* gone back for the car and then where would I be?"

The woman held up her hand. "Alright. I suppose it's okay. Mildred here can take you up to your sister's room." She turned her stare on the woman in pink scrubs, who was presumably a nurse. "But make sure it's alright with the sister first."

"Of course." And Mildred took Sam's arm and led her out of the office and down the corridor further into the hospital.

Sam let herself deflate some. "I'm sorry for being so flustered—I just can't believe something has happened to Kirin. How bad is she? It can't be too bad if she's able to talk? Can it?"

Mildred shook her head. "I really shouldn't discuss her condition with you—not until we know for sure you're family. But she can talk for herself."

Sam smiled, and it was genuine. She needed Kirin awake and able to understand everything Sam had to say.

Mildred led the way to an elevator. Inside, she pushed the button for the third floor. Sam would have thought the lift was only for the patients since it was only a five-story building—her effort to seem out-of-sorts must've made more of an impression than she'd intended.

Sam held her watch in front of her face, checking the time in an obvious fashion. "I feel so silly. At least I'm wearing my watch and my shoes." She tried a weak, trembling smile as Bailey had suggested. She held the watch out for Mildred to see. "Can that even be the right time?"

The nurse looked at the watch and nodded. "It's right—and it looks exactly like that watch of your sister's. Why do you both wear a man's watch? And the same one?"

The image of Harold as she last saw him helped Sam feel sad. "Our father—he gave each of us one just like his. Now we wear them to remember him by." That was stretching the truth past the breaking point, but it might be as close as this woman could understand anyway. "Mine has an engraving on the back. LD—3. Loving Daughter, and I'm the third."

Mildred shook her head. "So why does *she* have two of those same watches?"

"She wears our father's watch now all the time—she got it after his death. She carries her own with her as well." Sam shook her head. "But not her ID."

Mildred nodded, her face filled with sympathy as they stepped off the elevator. "We locked up your sister's belongings, most of them, for safekeeping. But at least she still has the watch she was wearing with her. She clearly values it a lot."

"You probably can't say, but I bet her purse held nothing but the watch and some cash. She doesn't like banks. So I'm glad you're keeping everything safe for her."

Sam followed the nurse down several hallways to a separate wing, where they stopped in front of the door to room 414.

Mildred held up a hand. "Stay right here for a moment while I make sure it's okay." Opening the door and leaving it open, the nurse stepped into a large, pleasant private room. Sam listened in.

Mildred entered with, "You're looking better."

Kirin's voice, "Is that some kind of joke?"

"No, dear—I understand you're upset, but your strength is returning. That's good."

"What will be *good* will be getting plastic surgery to fix this. And soon."

"And you'll need to be in good health before the doctor will perform that—regardless of how much money you have. Now, your sister's come looking for you. She's concerned, and I'm sure you want to see her. But don't let her tire you out. And just buzz the nurses' station if you need anything."

There was a long pause. If anything more was said Sam didn't hear it, but a moment later Mildred marched out of the room. "Now, don't wear her out. She needs her rest."

Sam nodded without saying a word and stalked on in to get her first look at Kirin's condition. The woman was propped up in bed with bandages over most of what could be seen, even over her left eye, and one of her legs was in a cast. She didn't appear pleased to see Sam, but that was to be expected.

Kirin glared out of the one eye. "Looking for my jewelry? The cash? They've got it locked in a safe, and you're not getting your hands on any of it."

"I'm not interested in the jewels or the money." Neither did Sam think them Kirin's, but she wasn't going to argue about that. "I did want to see what shape you're in."

"Come to gloat, is that it?" Even lying there in the hospital bed, Kirin still had her long, luxurious black hair, the alabaster skin and fine, classic bone structure—what could be seen of it.

"If you hadn't been trying to escape justice for the crimes you've committed, you'd not be here."

"Next you'll be telling me that *this* is justice— well, let me tell *you* something. I have all the money I'll need for the best plastic surgeons. They'll make me as good as new." Kirin snorted. "How *did* you follow me? I thought I'd left you far behind."

Sam smiled. "This was just a bump in the road to you?"

Kirin glared back at her. "Don't imagine you're going to finish the job. I've got my finger on the call button, and I'm strong enough to fend you off until help comes. Then you'd be in big trouble."

"I didn't come to kill you. I came to offer you a second chance. To make a deal."

Kirin snorted again. "You have nothing to offer me. Next time I Travel, I'll just make sure you're a long way away. Or dead."

"I don't think so." Sam's smile was grim as she removed her watch. "Our watches look exactly the same, so don't bother calling the nurse. I made sure to give Mildred a good look at mine." As she talked, Sam swapped her watch for the one on the bedside table. "The only difference between them is something they wouldn't even understand."

"You won't get away with this."

Sam ignored that. "Now, this is my offer, and I suggest you take it, since you can no longer Travel. And you no longer have access to the trust fund."

"I'll get that back from you. I swear."

Sam ignored that, too. "You could allow me to take you back to the others and answer for what you have done."

"You don't think I'd possibly go along with *that*. I'll stay in the past where no one can touch me."

Sam held up a hand. "I didn't imagine you'd go along with that. Not now. Someday you may *want* to atone for your actions, though."

Kirin narrowed her eye in suspicion. "So what's your offer then?"

"Just this. Keep your ill-gotten gains and try to live and be happy. If you can. I won't pursue you anymore."

"That's it?"

"Without a leader device, you'll have to answer to the contemporary authorities if you commit any further crimes."

Kirin's unbandaged eye twitched as she tried to glare Sam down. Sam stared straight back.

Silence stretched between them until Kirin decided to speak. "Now *you* have access to the trust, you can Travel. Take my advice and only Travel to the past. Because *I* will pursue *you*. With the money I have and the knowledge to invest it, I can still make myself incredibly wealthy. I'll be able to hire people to hunt you down."

Sam was taken aback by the bitterness in Kirin's voice. "I'm not worried about your wealth and what it can do. Neither am I interested in using the trust funds to try to get rich like you. And I'm not afraid of you."

"You should be. If you stay in this time or show up while I'm alive, I'll find you. And I'll give you the same thing I gave Harold." The woman laughed. "I may even make arrangements so that after I'm dead and gone, there'll still be a price on your head."

Sam was glad she'd kept Bailey's presence a secret. She would need that advantage—because she believed Kirin would do what she said. "I'm giving you the chance to end this now. I said I won't pursue you and I won't. But if you come after me, you'll have only yourself to blame for whatever happens."

"Get out."

Taking a last look at the woman, Sam left without another word. She ran into Mildred of the pink scrubs further down the corridor and walked with the nurse to the elevator.

While they waited, Mildred took a good look at Sam's face. "As bad as that?"

Which was when Sam realized that she was crying. She rubbed the tears away with the back of her hand and punched the elevator button again. She'd been through so much. It was just that this was the last straw, wearing her down to the nub.

She summoned a smile for the nurse. "I'm fine. But my sister—you may be able to fix the scars on the outside, but how can you heal the ones on the inside?"

Mildred shook her head. And as Sam was getting onto the elevator, she heard a warning. "They'll be waiting for you to fill out some forms—"

The closing doors cut off the rest, but Sam was grateful. When she stepped out on the ground floor, she started looking around for another exit, one that wouldn't take her out through the lobby but rather avoided the office lady in her flowery dress.

Sam found a side entrance and slipped out and kept her head down. She circled the building looking for Bailey. Of course she found him sitting up straight on the wooden bench with his eyes fixed on the front entrance of the hospital, watching for her to come out. She veered wide and approached him from behind.

"We're both still alive."

If she'd hoped to see the man jump or start, she would have been disappointed. He just stood and turned to look at her. "So what did happen?"

She loosed a long sigh. She wanted to sit down on the bench he'd just vacated and not get up. But she didn't.

"I got Harold's Travel device back—swapped it with my own. And I told Kirin that I won't be chasing her anymore."

"So that's it?"

"She swore to come after me. Hire people, hunt me down for the rest of her days." *And then some.*

"So what do we do?"

Sam looked up at him and smiled. "We make preparations. Kirin has a lot of recovering to do, so that gives us some time. But she'll be busy making her own plans."

Bailey grimaced. "We don't have any idea what those plans might be. How will she come after us?"

Sam's smile was thin. "Not us. Me. She doesn't know about you, and with those helper watches she can only track me now. At least that was how they were supposed to work. Since we can't rely on that, you'll have to stick close to me so we can preserve that advantage. And I'll need you there by my side when she does attack."

"Her advantage is all that money, so we'll need resources of our own. We had better get back to the city and visit the bank."

"The best resource I have is you, Bailey. You've got the experience and skills to handle whatever she comes at me with. Help me make plans."

He grunted. "Right now we barely have enough for a bus ticket back into New York City. At least I can carry you to the station."

Sam shook her head. "I can walk." She started strolling in what she hoped was the right direction, Bailey by her side. "By the way, the answer came to me—why we Traveled with Kirin at such a distance. I was hoping you could explain to me how it actually works."

"You know what the answer is but you don't understand it?"

"Because it's the only thing that makes sense."

The moan of a strong wind came from her partner, and Sam figured that was an expression of his exasperation with her.

She squinted into the distance and tried to say what she knew. "Kirin still had her own helper device on her all the while she was using Harold's to Travel. I don't understand how these things work, but her having two devices must be responsible for the two of us Traveling with her."

Bailey plodded along. "I don't understand how they work, either. But since the helper devices generate a kind of field of their own that's supposed to merge with the main one, it must have combined in a different way with both of them together like that. That's my best guess. It's not my area."

"Mine either. But that must be it. The helper device did its thing when she used Harold's to Travel, making the field bigger or wider. Or whatever. And our devices did their thing."

"That must be it." *TB*

Chapter 13

The Former Preacher's Tale

July 29th, 2000 The Bronx (on I-87)

ANYA sat in air-conditioned comfort in the back seat of the hired car as it glided serenely along the busy highway—and she was sweating. *This isn't like me*. She couldn't remember the last time a sudden crisis had caused her this kind of anxiety. Maybe because *this* had been building for three weeks— she'd seen it coming, dreaded it, and yet failed to do anything to stop it.

Of course, it wasn't like Turner to call in a panic trying to explain the problem with incoherent rambling. Nye couldn't just be *gone*. Her helper device couldn't Travel on its own, and it was impossible for another leader to come and leave again so soon.

Anya would be better equipped to deal with the situation once she understood what had happened. She certainly couldn't rely on the little she'd gathered from her flustered helper. Once she found the man, she would get Turner to make sense.

She tried finding her peace. The problem was past preventing—she needed to do what she always did in a crisis. Deal with it. She'd left Tate at home and could depend on him to take care of everything there, so she needn't worry about that.

Staring out the window into the dark, she realized she should be grateful—that they'd gotten the phone installed before this emergency and that she had been able to find a hired car in the middle of the night to take her into the city. She should be glad to have the resources to pay for this kind of help, when she didn't have the ID to rent a car. She ought not to be driving in the state she was in anyway.

She wondered if they were getting close. Looking up into the rearview mirror and the reflection of the driver's impassive face, she asked. "Is the hotel much farther?"

"We're about to cross into Harlem, so it'll be another fifteen or twenty minutes, mam."

"Thank you." She sighed and sank back into the seat. If only Nye hadn't insisted on spending almost all of her days in the city. If only Turner hadn't been so willing to chaperone her on those trips. *If only.*

Anya and Tate had been happy enough to enjoy the comfort of their new home, to spend their time reading newspapers and listening to the radio, even watching terrible television in the name of research. Of course, the best part had been bicycling around their rural neighborhood and meeting the natives.

Nye, however, wasn't interested in interviewing subjects. She wasn't satisfied with the idea of filtering information from media sources. She wanted to make hands-on observations of the city whose ruins had always fascinated her, and she had to be there doing that to the exclusion of all else. And every day the girl spent in the city, Anya worried a little more.

She couldn't deny the trips into the city when a chaperone was available, and Turner hadn't hesitated to volunteer at every request. Which meant the two of them had been spending most of their time in the city. More potential for some kind of trouble.

Now that trouble had arrived.

Of course, she'd been aware of Nye's tendency toward obsessing over her work and not acting with prudence—it was why Anya had insisted on a chaperone for the girl. But Turner had his own research and work to do for the team. He couldn't supervise Nye every single minute. There had been reason to suspect a problem might develop, and now it had.

Absorbed in her thoughts, the time slipped by, and Anya was surprised to look out the window and see they were pulling up in front of the Hotel Ngaio —this was the place Turner and Nye were using as a base of operations in the city.

Anya was already opening the door before the vehicle had come to a complete stop. She wouldn't wait for the driver or the doorman to open it for her.

The driver looked over his shoulder as she was sliding out. "What did you want me to do, mam?"

She paused. "This will probably only take ten or fifteen minutes. I don't know yet where I'll want to go after."

The driver nodded. "Then I'll just keep circling the block until I see you're ready, mam."

Anya almost ran into the hotel, where she found Turner pacing back and forth in the lobby, waiting. As soon as he noticed her, he rushed over. When he opened his mouth to start explaining, she shushed the man, grabbed his elbow, and steered him over to a sofa standing against the far wall of the lobby. So they could have some privacy.

She sat them both down and started things in a quiet voice. "Now why don't you try and state exactly what happened, with clear details so I can actually understand you. And keep your voice low."

He took several long, deep breaths and calmed himself before speaking. "I was working late, trying to get my website properly set up. It was getting on toward midnight when I remembered Nye."

Anya kept from shaking her head. Turner's supervision had been more lax than she'd realized and this was the result. "You were working here in your hotel room? Where was Nye, the last you knew?"

The man shook his head and blushed. "I wasn't here. Ms. Dervan had volunteered to help me. She has an incredible computer workstation, and I was in her apartment while she was teaching me what I needed to know."

"There's no need to blush, Turner. I trust you wouldn't be doing anything inappropriate. And I'm glad the woman is helping. Your website will be one more way the others can find their way back to us. But what about Nye?"

"She had been roaming around the city somewhere, but she'd promised to be back at the hotel before dark. She knew I'd come searching for her if she failed to return, and drag her back in the middle of her research. Because I've had to do that several times. But I thought she'd learned her lesson."

Anya snorted. "This is Nye we're talking about. It's not that she doesn't know what she ought to do. She always has. She just gets so absorbed she loses track, and loses her good sense."

Turner's face flushed deeper red. "I'm sorry. I guess I got too involved myself. Anyway, it was late, and before I headed back to the hotel I checked the locator app to see if she was in that direction."

Anya frowned. "You must've gotten some kind of a bead on her."

On their first foray into the city after the move to Little Piece, Turner and Nye had discovered that with Anya's leader device that far away, their own helper devices had defaulted to track each other. It should have made it that much easier for Turner to supervise his charge.

Turner stared off into the distance. "It pointed to the north. Even though I was on the Upper West Side already, I assumed Nye had wandered that far and stayed out late again. So I set off to track her down, like I had before. I ended up taking a taxi to the north end of the Bronx without it ever changing direction or turning to a blip."

Anya nodded. "At which point you must have realized that it was pointing at me up in Chickadee County."

"I admit I panicked then. I used that cell phone I'd gotten for emergencies and woke you up and I got you to come. Then I realized it could just be a bug in the programming. The locator app might've returned to its normal function—stopped tracking the nearest device and gone back to pointing to the leader, like we thought it was supposed to."

"So you came back here, to the hotel?"

"I had to wait for you, since you said you were on your way, but I also hoped to find Nye waiting."

Anya sighed. "Because if it was just a bug in the watch programming, Nye could've been in the hotel all along." And Turner would've been panicking at nothing. The man was overly conscious of how he'd fallen short of his responsibility. "I take it you didn't find her here, though."

Turner shook his head. "If the problem is with the locator app, I have no way to find out where she is. So I'm glad I called you. With your device, you can track her down, and we can discover what kind of trouble I've allowed her to get into."

Anya brought up the locator screen on her own watch. Turner showed up as a blip in the middle, of course, and the red bar pointed to the north. That might be pointing at Tate or Nye. If that wasn't the girl to the north, then the next logical assumption would be that she had Traveled, if that weren't impossible.

Anya looked hard at Turner. "If another Traveler, a leader, had shown up in this time—had stayed around long enough for their device to recharge and leave again—wouldn't one of you have noticed?"

Turner nodded and then exhaled in relief. "I've messed up, I know, but it's not been that bad. Until tonight, I'd been checking my locator screen pretty much every hour. Except when I'm sleeping. Tonight was the first time I'd let it go longer, because I got wrapped up in my work. Just like Nye."

Anya smiled. "Maybe it's contagious. But the important point is—if you were checking that often, you would've had to notice sometime if your watch indicated a direction different from where you knew Nye to be. Another leader in the city? Today?"

Turner shook his head. "No. And you're right, I'd have noticed. It was only for several hours late this evening, last evening now, that I got so distracted I forgot to check."

"So Nye didn't Travel. Presumably."

The man was slowly getting himself back into a clear state of mind. He sat straighter and stared at Anya. "What then? How did she disappear? How are we supposed to find her if we can't use the locator app?"

"I can only think of two reasons why her signal might have gone dark. One is if her watch had been destroyed—let's hope it's not that, because I don't even want to think of what that might mean for Nye. If it's the other, then we only have to wait for her to show up on the screen again."

Turner's mouth had started to gape. "What was the second possibility? I missed that."

Anya gave him a hard look. He really was running himself ragged, to the point he couldn't think straight. "Because I didn't say. I'd rather not. Anyway, the car I hired to come here has been circling the block for a while, and we'd better go."

Turner bounded off the sofa and started for the doors, then came back as Anya stood. "Shouldn't I say here at the hotel? In case she comes back?

"If she could have, she'd have returned by now. It's not long before dawn." Anya shook her head. "I think you'd better stay and get some sleep, though. You clearly need to rest."

Turner nodded and started to walk away, then he came back again. "I couldn't possibly sleep, not until I know if she's alright."

So Anya walked out of the lobby to the curb with Turner following behind. It was only a few minutes before she saw the car approaching from around the corner and waved. The driver pulled up and Turner ran and opened the door for her.

After they had both settled in the back seat, the driver looked in the rearview mirror at Anya. "Now where do you want to go, mam? Back home?"

"You can drive north for a while, if you please. But I don't think we're going home." She couldn't imagine what he was thinking about all of this, but that was the least of her worries.

She kept checking her watch. If the locator was pointing at Nye, it should switch before they left the city. It was likely Tate and they'd be turning around and looking for Nye. Anya scowled at her helper. "Do you at least have some idea what area of the city she'd been working in last night?"

Turner sighed. "She'd been concentrating on Midtown and staying fairly close to the hotel, but I think that was because she was working her way out in some kind of grid pattern."

"You'd better try to get a little nap if you can. This may take some time."

He scrunched back into the seat and let his head flop back with his eyes wide open. If that were the best he could do for rest, it would have to be enough. After several minutes of eerie quiet in the insulation and isolation of the car interior, Anya began to fidget. She kept checking her watch and trying to keep her mind off of Nye by staring out at the city as they rode along. It didn't help.

At some point Anya noticed the first hint of day, as a few weak rays managed to filter over the horizon and between all the buildings. She checked her locator screen for the umpteenth time and saw a red bar at the bottom. *South.* North *had* been Tate.

For the space of one unusually loud heartbeat, she froze. Then she leaned forward to speak to the driver. "We want to head back to the south. I'll give you further directions when we get closer."

She'd hoped to avoid waking Turner, if the man were somehow asleep like that, but he lifted up his head and looked at her. "You've got her?"

Anya nodded. "We'll soon find out what kind of trouble she's gotten herself into."

The driver must've been thinking stranger and stranger things as she kept checking her watch and navigating him through the streets of the city toward an unknown destination. But he didn't say a word. She was liking the man more and more.

She finally saw them approach an assortment of buildings, varying in size and age, but all large and institutional. She pointed them out to the driver. "We're headed there. It's a hospital." Of a size and scope Anya had only read about in history books.

The driver nodded. "Yes, mam. I assume you're just visiting?"

"Yes. A friend."

The driver took a left into the complex and began weaving through the buildings as Anya kept a close eye on her watch. When the bar changed to a blip, she asked the man to stop in front of the nearest building. Nye was inside.

The sign on the outside said it was for 'behavioral health' and Anya could translate that into what it really meant—Nye had been acting her usual self.

Anya opened the door and started to slide out, then turned back to the driver. "This might take a very long time."

The driver pointed at a big parking garage. "I'll get something to eat and park there to wait."

Anya nodded and finished climbing out of the car, her weary helper following. "Come on, now."

As she stalked up to the entrance, Anya tried to imagine how difficult this could be. She glanced at Turner. "This will be tough, so don't say anything. Just try to look handsome."

She had to admit to herself, though, that even Turner's most effective charm would likely be insufficient to this challenge. Maybe some camaraderie between nurses would do the trick. *But I won't hold my breath.*

Inside the lobby, Anya saw a sally port leading back to the wards, but the only approach to anyone was through a thick plastic barrier, translucent with tiny holes to allow sound to penetrate. A woman sitting behind that protection looked like a clerk of some sort.

Turner put his hand on Anya's arm to stop her. "If we've got the signal back, why not just Travel Nye out of this place?"

"Aside from the fact that she's far enough away that the separation factor might land her on a boat in the Atlantic, she may have had to hide her watch. If she's not wearing it, all we'd accomplish would be to Travel the watch where it might never be found."

Anya walked up to speak to the woman behind the plastic. "I'm looking for a friend who ended up here, sometime last night. Her name is Nye."

The woman didn't even bother to look at Anya. "I'm sorry, but I can't give out patient information."

Anya sighed. "I don't need *information.* I need my friend, and you have her."

Now the woman looked, squinting through the thick plastic. "If she was admitted last night, that might have been for a seventy-two hour evaluation. You'd better hope that's the case. After that period, she'd either be committed or released. You'll have to wait to find out which it is, though."

Anya took a deep breath to hold her peace. "I'm a retired nurse, and I can tell you Nye isn't insane." She tried to smile. "She's a little scattered, and a bit obsessive, but not crazy."

"We don't like to use terms like that, which you should know." The woman sighed and rubbed the bridge of her nose between her thumb and forefinger. "Look, there's simply nothing to be done until the doctors make their evaluation. We'll release her if she's not a danger to herself or others."

Anya rubbed the back of her neck. This was going to be the start of a very long day. She glanced behind her and saw that Turner had disappeared. She looked at the empty plastic chairs bolted to the floor and turned back to the woman.

"I'll just wait here for my friend then. They'll realize soon enough she's no danger."

The woman shook her head. "You don't understand. If she was brought in last night for a seventy-two hour eval, she's got at least sixty hours to go."

The woman bent her head to attend to some papers, as if that were the end of the matter.

Anya sighed. "I'm sure you're very busy. Why not take my word that there's nothing much wrong with Nye—take a quick look at her to be sure, and then let me get her out of your hair?"

"I'm sorry. We *are* busy. Two doctors have to see her and sign off on whatever determination they make. And I'm not going to try and tell them what that should be. You'll just have to wait."

"*I'm* sorry if I'm being difficult. I'll wait." She went to one of those empty hard plastic chairs and sat and tried to think, but it was hard in that drab, oppressive environment. Hopefully Turner would return soon and keep her company.

She didn't think it had been long since leaning back her head to stare at the ceiling when she felt someone sit down beside her. It had to be Turner. She rolled her head a little to the side and her eyes listed over to confirm it.

"Where have you been?"

"I wanted some privacy when I talked to Verity on the phone. Ms. Dervan. This situation seemed like it might call for some extra help. So she's sending us some."

"Help?" Whatever kind of assistance the efficient Ms. Dervan might be sending, it would likely be effective. Hopefully it would arrive soon.

Anya let her eyes close again and let her head rest back against the brick wall behind her. "Since *you* can't rest, why don't you be helpful and phone Tate to tell him what's going on? And tell him not to worry."

She felt Turner lean forward and walk away and then all she could do was wait. For Turner to come back. For Ms. Dervan's help to arrive. For the psychiatrists to hopefully realize that Nye wasn't nuts, but that depended a lot on the girl herself.

When a hand gently shook her shoulder, Anya's eyes popped open. She must've drifted off, despite the circumstances and the setting, but she'd needed it. She lifted her head, alert and ready.

She placed her hand over Turner's on her shoulder. "Thank you."

Then she noticed the gray-haired man in a gray suit lurking behind her helper. She stood to greet this man and noticed how expensive his attire was— it might be someone in authority. Or Ms. Dervan's idea of assistance.

He had a salt-and-pepper mustache and a wry grin. "Excuse me. Miss Anya? My name is Crispin Hollingsworth, and I'm your attorney."

She blinked. "I didn't know I had a lawyer."

"Technically I've been retained by the trust, but I understand you'll be the one paying my bill, so it's your interests I'm representing."

Anya felt a deep relief. She didn't know what he could or couldn't do to help, but she couldn't think of anything better. "Did Turner describe the situation?"

Mr. Hollingsworth gave her a slight shake of his head. "He told me a little. Very little. Not that I'd need, or even want to know, everything." Then he gave her a meaningful look.

"I see." At least Turner had been discreet, and apparently this lawyer wanted her to watch herself. It was nice to see her helper returning to his usual competence, and if the lawyer needed more details than she gave him, he could always ask. "I'll try to give you the gist of the situation, but there are some things I may not be able to share with you." *Things that might get me locked up along with Nye.*

The lawyer combed his mustache with a finger. "Don't worry about that. I'm used to clients withholding. As long as you don't *lie*, we'll be fine."

She nodded. "I won't lie." She explained about what they surmised had happened to Nye, without any explanation for why they thought it. "Now, is there any way to get her out of here? Soon?"

"It depends. I can see a number of difficulties. You say she didn't have any ID on her, so it will be hard to prove you have any right to even know she's here. But as an attorney, I can represent her interests without having to prove anything. But it would be helpful if we could establish her identity. Do you have anything that can do that?"

Anya shook her head. "I'm afraid not."

"Can you get some, or is she illegal?" Mr. Hollingsworth must've seen the confusion on her face. "Is she a citizen? Was she born here?"

She chose her words with care. "If you mean to ask if she was born in a geographic area you would call United States territory, then the answer is yes. Unfortunately that can't be proven."

The lawyer sighed. "Well, I was told you won't have any trouble paying my fee. And dealing with difficult problems is what I get paid for."

"I don't know what Ms. Dervan told you, but I and my friends are all researchers for a non-profit organization. The trust finances our operations. If you represent the trust, then by extension you also represent the organization Nye works for."

"You're bright. Maybe you should have my job. Of course, that was the tactic I intended to take, but it would be easier if I could prove Miss Nye's identity. Can you at least tell me her full name?"

She shook her head. "It's just Nye. But you're saying there's something you can do to get her out?"

Mr. Hollingsworth grinned. "I can. Your friend is a researcher—can you give me any more?"

Anya considered it. "She's a graduate student of archaeology. I can't say where."

"Very mysterious."

Anya continued. "She gets obsessive about her work, but she's not nuts. But it's probably related to how she ended up here. And when she's absorbed in her research she can sound strange, but she should be able to convince the doctors she's alright. Since she'll not be engaged in her studies in here."

The lawyer nodded as he paid close attention to everything Anya said. "I'll know more details once I've talked to someone in charge, but for now I want you two to stay here. I'll report back when I know something."

With that he marched over to the woman sitting behind her screen and showed *his* identification and said something Anya couldn't hear. Following that short discussion, he was buzzed back into the little office area.

Anya sat back down again. She'd gotten what rest she needed, but she had nothing to do now but wait. Again. Turner sat down beside her, so at least she had company in her idleness now.

She turned to him. "Your Ms. Dervan certainly came through for us with just the help we needed. Remind me to thank her."

Turner blushed. "I'd already mentioned to her some of the problems we have encountered, lacking legal identification. She'd raised the possibility of using a lawyer as a proxy for some of those things in a similar way to how you went through the bank to buy the house. So when I called, I asked her to go ahead and retain the best attorney she could find."

Anya smiled at him. "It's alright. We'd have to deal with these issues at some point anyway. And I'm sure Ms. Dervan will be discreet."

"We can trust Verity." Her helper gave a little cough into his hand. "But there are still a number of things a lawyer can't do for us. I think we'll need to find a way to get some proper identification if we're going to stay and do research."

Verity, again. If she didn't know any better, Anya might think Turner was getting too familiar with the woman. The man *was* becoming independent. Something Anya should probably be grateful for, as he had a good head on his shoulders and kept proving it. He just needed to remember how to follow her instructions.

She patted him on the shoulder and settled in for a long wait, but before she knew it, their lawyer had returned to the lobby and crossed to where they were sitting. "Let's take matters one at a time. It's not all bad news. First, your friend *is* here."

Anya squinted at the lawyer. "We already knew that."

"Yes, but had you gotten them to admit the fact? We needed them to do that before we could do anything else."

"I'm sorry. You were saying?"

"Then I found out why and how she was admitted. Supposedly your friend was 'harassing' some workers at the New York Coliseum demolition site. The police were called, and they decided from her behavior and some comments she made that they should bring her in for a psychiatric evaluation."

Anya rolled her eyes. She could just imagine the kind of behavior Nye had demonstrated. "It's likely all true. But what now? Will we have to wait the full seventy-two hours? Is there any chance they might actually commit her?"

The lawyer shook his head. "Not if I can help it. They wouldn't let me see her medical records, of course, but I'm told she was evaluated by one doctor when she was admitted. His report was equivocal, so it depends on what the second psychiatrist says. But the first doctor will rubber stamp whatever the other recommends."

Anya didn't need to be told that last part. She'd worked with doctors long enough. "What now?"

"I've had a little chat with the hospital administrator. Officially nothing's changed—but, without saying your friend is getting any kind of preferential treatment, the second doctor will happen to review her case soon. No one is going to insist on a particular verdict, but that psychiatrist will understand the administration's *feelings*."

Anya grinned. "But how did you convince them to arrange things like that?"

Mr. Hollingsworth combed his mustache with his finger. "No one wants to be dragged into court if they can help it. And I have a certain reputation. I expect your friend will be released and returned to you shortly. Unless this Nye does something stupid, which you tell me is unlikely."

"Thank you. This is the best I could've hoped for." They certainly had gotten their money's worth —depending on what his bill was.

"I've done all I can do, and it should be fine now. But you're paying me by the hour—if you want me to sit around with you and wait…"

"No, indeed. Thank you again for what you've done. And we'll contact you if it turns out we need more help."

The lawyer grinned. "I sincerely hope you don't, Miss Anya. I have enough money as it is." With that he tipped an imaginary hat at her and walked out of the hospital.

Turner looked from the lawyer leaving to her. "I'm still curious why we lost Nye's signal."

Anya smiled to herself. "At some point she had to realize they might take her possessions, and she wouldn't want to lose her watch, even temporarily, or let the wrong people get too close a look at it. I suspect she swallowed it."

Turner's eyes widened. "That would be enough to keep the locator from tracking her?"

"Probably not normally, though it *would* cause interference. Since the device charges off the body's electrical field. But remember that Nye's body has absorbed abnormally high levels of radiation."

"So how did the signal return?"

Before Anya could decide how she'd answer his question, the sally port that led back to the wards opened and Nye came trotting out toward them.

Mr. Hollingsworth must have scared the hospital administrator good, and Anya really didn't care how he'd done that. It was just good to see Nye.

The girl came up to them beaming, and thankfully wearing her watch. "That was interesting."

Anya shook her head in wonder. "You enjoyed your experience, did you?"

"I wouldn't say enjoyed. It *was* educational."

"I hope your Travel device still works properly. At least it did enough for us to track you here."

Nye shrugged. "It looked alright when I washed it off. A little worn, but it seemed to function fine."

Anya smiled at the girl. "That would've been the acids in your stomach."

Turner interjected. "Now what? Back to the hotel, or all the way back to Chickadee County?"

Anya considered. "We'll return home, for long enough to rest a bit and get things squared away. I want to put some distance between us and this incident. Cut the summer short and go to next year."

Turner definitely did not look happy. "I still haven't finished getting the web site set up. At least let me leave Ms. Dervan a message."

Nye piped up. "We're leaving?"

Anya kept her voice low. No one was around to hear, but they were still standing in a mental hospital. "I hope you got enough of a baseline to start, because I want to skip ahead to two thousand one. We'll make next summer extra long to make up for cutting this one short."

She glanced at Turner. "Leave your message, but finishing the website can wait until next year."

Chapter 14
Abandoned

July 30th, 2000 Midtown Manhattan

MATT pushed through the side exit, pulling Page along behind and trying not to rush out of the building. It was night, with bright lights all around, and warm. *When are we?* She had said she was aiming for the summer of two thousand.

Page stopped and stood her ground as soon as they were out on the sidewalk. She looked down at her watch. "It's two and a half years in the future—I doubt they're still looking for us." She fiddled with her device a little more. *Finding her friends.*

Matt dropped her hand with some reluctance. They'd been so close when they'd Traveled, he had failed to notice any separation when they'd arrived.

"I'd rather not be found inside while you're carrying *that* bag, and stuffed with cash."

Page rolled her eyes. "Both receipts are dated from the past, now—they won't be taken for forgeries." Apparently forgetting they'd left the receipt for the bag two and a half years in the past. "Anyway, I'm tired of shopping."

"I'm not surprised. I suppose we should get you a hotel room for the night. You can find the others and go shopping tomorrow, if you still want to."

"I *am* tired."

Matt looked down at the watch he was wearing and frowned. "Two and a half years in the future, you said. It's the thirtieth of July—I've been gone for a whole month. People will be wondering."

"Close enough. I've returned you to your own time, your own life. Now I need to get back to mine. But before I do—" Page reached into her pocket and pulled out Matt's billfold and handed it to him. "I imagine you'll need that."

He found he couldn't feel irritated with her casual dismissal of his lost month. "I thought we were supposed to come through at the same time of day, but it's several hours later."

"Because at the same hour in summer, it would still have been light out. The bias is to help prevent a feeling of disorientation from a change in sensory input."

"Like jet lag."

Page gave him a blank look.

Matt sighed. "When you board a plane in the morning and then travel half the day, only you land and it's still morning, or the middle of the night."

"Oh, airplanes."

The way she said it made him wonder again—what that future world she came from was like. He'd have to continue with her if he hoped to find out the answers. Of course, he had other reasons to stick by her.

He'd known this moment was coming, and now it was here. But he wasn't ready to let go. "Are you going to search for your friends right now?"

She stared at him for a long moment, but it was too dark to see the wheels turning behind her eyes. "I think I want to find that room and rest for a while, before I do anything."

"Then why don't I help you search for a hotel. I should probably continue to escort you anyway, as long as you're carrying around all that cash. Until you've got your real helpers back at least."

"You don't have to do that. Contrary to the impression I've given you, I *can* take care of myself."

Matt pressed his lips together to hold back the comment that immediately sprang to mind. "You need a nice hotel, one where you won't have to worry about carrying that cash. You'll need me to use my ID and credit card for that kind of place." *If my card hasn't been canceled by now.*

Page nodded. "I'd appreciate your help. But in the morning, I'll go to the bank first thing. I'll deposit most of this money into my account and see about getting one of those debit card things. Then you won't feel you have to protect me, and you can get back to your own life."

Matt grinned. "It's difficult getting away from you. I wonder if that will do it." He also wondered when she was going to demand her watch back. It had been a while since she'd pressed him on it, and now if she would be leaving him behind, she'd need it back. And he was out of excuses for holding on to it. "For now, you're still *my* responsibility."

"Well then, take me to a good hotel. And I told you I'm tired, so make it one close by."

"We're between Broadway and Park Avenue—why not just close your eyes and point? Or try the nearest first, until we find you something?"

"Alright, Matt. It's your city."

Page walked wearily beside him into the plush lobby of the closest hotel he could see. He gestured at a comfortable couch. "Why don't you relax while I find out if I can get you a room?"

She nodded without a word and plopped down on one of the big red leather sofas with her bag sitting next to her. He hurried over to approach the desk clerk and discover if they had any vacancies. They did.

Matt took out his credit card and slid it across the counter, praying it wouldn't be declined. "Two single rooms, if they're available, and next to each other if you can."

The man clicked away on his computer. "I can give you two single rooms on the same floor. That's the best I can do, sir."

"That'll be fine."

The clerk programmed the card keys for both rooms and handed them over with the receipt to be signed and a folder with the record of the reservation. Matt slid his own key into his wallet together with his credit card. He walked back over to Page and handed her the other.

"Room 404. And if you want to put your bag in the hotel safe, I'm sure that clerk would help you—but you might want to take out some cash first."

Page nodded. "I already took a wad of bills and stuffed them in my pocket. You see? I can take care of myself and don't need you to do my thinking."

"You want your watch back now?"

"That's not necessary. I switched them when I was swapping the batteries. You never noticed how I was operating the watch on my own wrist?"

He'd been too distracted. It *was* her watch, but her trick still irked him. *So much for trust.*

Matt didn't know what to say. "I guess I'll stop by in the morning. In case you've not reunited with your friends yet and need an escort to the bank."

"If you feel you have to."

"I do. I don't want you trying to carry that cash alone through the city." *She swapped the watches.* ᵛᵏ⎦

Page smiled. "Then goodbye for now, Matt." ⌐⌐

"Alright, then. Good luck with your research." ʰᵉʳ watch

He turned and walked out of the lobby without looking back, leaving before she thought to ask for the other device. He stopped to think once he was out in the bright, busy night. There were things he should do before he returned to his room down the hall from Page. He wouldn't let her slip away from him, not yet.

And with the room nearby and the locator app on this watch he was wearing, he should be able to stick close to her.

Like Page, he wanted to lie down and rest. But first he needed to go back to the clinic he'd left only this morning, a month ago, and find out what had happened to him. Since that was a long, long walk, he decided to splurge on a taxi.

Before he tried hailing a cab, though, he had to check to make sure he understood how to work the tracking function on the helper device he now possessed. She had shown him, but that could've been another of her tricks.

Standing on the sidewalk, Matt switched to the locator screen. He saw the white blip that ought to correspond to where Page must have been making her way up to her room. Recalling the layout of the hotel, he estimated the size of the area that screen represented. Now he knew the range.

He was glad he'd taken that second room. He didn't have a plan yet, but he meant to Travel with Page whenever she left the present. So he had to try and stay close enough to be inside the field when it happened. But she wouldn't be leaving until midday tomorrow at the earliest, and he had things he needed to wrap up if he intended to abandon *this* life for one with Page. If she let him.

Matt hailed a taxi then, and after it was taking him away he checked the locator screen again and saw Page's blip had disappeared and a glowing red bar had lit up at the bottom. *South.*

Now he was comfortable with using this device to keep track of Page if he had to. He hoped it didn't come to that. In the morning, maybe she wouldn't have found her friends yet, or they'd not have found her, and he could escort her to the bank. And find some way to convince her to let him come along. If that meant shopping, even—eventually he'd figure out a way to extend their partnership.

Matt sat tense in the back of the cab all the way to the Empire City Clinic. He worried about Page, and he wondered what might've happened over the last month to his supposedly 'normal' life. After the driver had dropped him off, he stood outside soaking up the atmosphere.

It felt as if he'd been gone for years. In a sense he had. *And a lot can happen in a month.* He hoped Marcia hadn't changed shifts, though—a month ago she wouldn't have been working this late, and he'd rather not face her questions about what had happened that morning in the clinic.

Finally he took the plunge and entered. Walked right up to the receptionist he didn't know. "Please page Dr. Wallace."

The woman frowned up at him. "Dr. Wallace is busy. If you need help—"

"Just tell Harding his old friend Matt is here to see him."

She shook her head but grabbed the phone and called someone, repeating his message. She hung up and looked at him. "Dr. Wallace will see you in his office. It's down—"

"I know where it is. Thanks." Matt headed back through the small clinic's sterile white halls, trying not to think about the last time he was here.

He found Harding leaning against the jamb in his office doorway, waiting. They both grinned, but Matt saw the new wrinkles on his friend's forehead. *Stress.* The man *had* chosen to become a doctor.

"You're looking good for a ghost." With which remark, Harding ushered Matt into his stark, utilitarian office.

Matt perched on the metal stool that likely belonged in an examination room. "Is that your way of telling me I've been declared dead?"

"No such luck, I'm afraid." His friend plopped down hard in his cheap office chair and began swiveling back and forth. "It means Marcia's been going on about how you vanished into thin air right before her eyes. She's now convinced you were a specter all along. It *is* hard to believe you're real."

"And I suppose the patient I brought in never existed at all."

"Marcia's the only one who remembers seeing you with an attractive redhead." Harding chuckled. "She made a few notes but only wrote down a first name, so no one really believes her."

Matt frowned. "Sorry about that, Wall. I didn't exactly choose to leave the way I did."

"You know I hate that nickname."

"Why do you think I use it?"

His friend grabbed a pen off his desk and began twirling it in his fingers. "Your parents are worried —the poor people called me to try and get in touch with you, but what could I tell them?"

"Can I use your computer for a minute? I'd better e-mail them."

Harding nodded and rolled his chair across the floor to the other side of the room. "Nobody at the school is concerned about you, though." The man grinned. "You did lose your apartment. The landlord was quick to box up your belongings and rent the place to someone else. Who knows where your stuff is now?"

Matt shrugged. It was never a real home, and he'd nothing there of value—sentimental or otherwise. He stood and walked to the desk, hunching over the keyboard long enough to log in to his webmail account and send a short note to his parents. Then that much at least was finished.

He moved away and looked back at his friend. "I told them to call you if they have any questions. You can tell them I was no phantom."

"Thanks." Harding's smile was grim. "I take it you mean to disappear again?"

Matt nodded. He thought about Page at the hotel and how he should be headed back there. It had been easier to wrap things up here than he'd anticipated. "Only this time it's intentional."

His friend stood and flipped his pen over onto his desk and offered his hand. "I sure will miss you. Do you think you might drop back in again someday?"

Matt shook his friend's hand. "I've no idea what the future holds, Wall, or the past."

Matt walked out of that office, and hopefully out of his old life. Needing the exercise and in no rush to get back to the hotel in Midtown, he didn't bother trying to find a taxi—he just started walking.

If he managed to stay with Page, he had no idea where or when that would take him, so he might as well enjoy the sights and sounds of the city as if for the last time. Not that he'd miss it.

He stayed alert as he strode through the jungle, because it was just as wild as he'd tried to convince Page. It was a fascinating wilderness however, and thankfully tonight a calm one. *On the surface.*

When he passed through into a nicer neighborhood, he used his bank card to get out as much cash as it would let him. *It's a good thing I'm not dead, or the ATM wouldn't give me any money.*

He kept checking the locator as he walked along even though he didn't expect Page would be on the move. He imagined she'd be fast asleep. She could have started looking for her friends though, or gone shopping. *She's unpredictable.*

By the time he got back to the hotel he was not only tired, but thoroughly exhausted. He even took the elevator up to save his feet.

He paused in front of room 404 and checked to make sure she was safely inside. *Dead to the world, no doubt.* Then he trudged down the hall to his own room and collapsed on the bed.

A few minutes later he was startled awake by a ringing noise near his head. The hotel phone. Light was streaming in through the window because he'd not bothered to close the curtains.

Matt wondered if Page had checked her device and discovered where he was. She could be calling for her escort to the bank.

He grabbed the receiver while he tried to blink the sleep out of his eyes. "Hello?"

"Mr. Walker? Room 412?" Not Page's voice—someone official.

"That's me."

"Did you wish a longer stay? To keep one room or both? You understand we require guests to check out before eleven. But if you intend to stay..."

Matt was confused until he looked at his watch and saw it was already half past ten in the morning. "I'll keep both rooms another day if I can."

"Will you be having another guest, sir?"

Matt swung his feet over the bed and combed his free hand through his hair as his brain kicked into action. "Another? What about my friend Page in room 404?"

"I'm sorry, sir. I supposed you knew the young lady had checked out."

Checked out? He'd told her to expect him in the morning to see if she needed an escort to the bank. *What did she think when I failed to show?*

He said a quick thanks to the hotel clerk, hung up the phone, and started for the door. Not having undressed for bed, he was ready to go.

Page could have gone to the bank already. She could've reunited with her friends, then forgotten about him. As Matt darted out into the corridor and headed for the stairs, he realized he hadn't thought to ask *when* Page had checked out.

The bank wouldn't have opened until nine, so she might still be there. He hit the sidewalk outside and kept going. Since it was only a few blocks away, he'd probably get there faster on his long legs than by trying to catch a cab.

Matt weaved swiftly through the throngs on the street, hoping to arrive at the bank before Page had left. Which meant he arrived out of breath.

He didn't want to run into the bank like that, so he stopped outside the entrance and made himself cool down, relax. At least he'd meet her coming out if he hadn't already missed her. Then he remembered the locator.

This was what came from starting his day without coffee. His brain was slow to move. He looked down at the device on his wrist and checked Page's location. *South.* He didn't know how far south, but she wasn't in the bank.

Matt was torn. He wanted to turn right around and go after her. But he didn't know if she'd even been to the bank yet—she might be headed in this direction even now.

His mind made up, Matt plunged into the chilly air-conditioned lobby and looked around. When he saw a familiar face from their previous visit, he was pleased and smiled at the secretary sitting far at the back at a wide desk. She didn't seem to notice.

He walked over and didn't waste time exchanging greetings. "Has she been here? Did she make it okay?"

Ms. Dervan glared at him. "If you mean Page, she's been and gone already. You missed her."

"Did she say where she was going?" He had the locator device to track her by, but if she was headed any distance, it would help to know where.

"She said you stood her up."

Matt sighed. Women sure stuck together on occasions like this. "I overslept."

"You men are always making excuses. Except for when you don't even bother to do that. Go find her yourself."

She was right of course—he should be out looking for Page now. She might already be in trouble. "Thank you."

With a smile and a nod, he turned and walked across the lobby and out into the street. He checked the watch again and headed south. If he'd not been in such a rush, he could've used the device to start tracking Page from the hotel and saved himself time and energy. But that was past.

At least he still had several hours or more until she could Travel again. She'd probably want to wait the full twenty-four hours needed for her device to finish recharging.

He bet she would spend that time shopping. Or looking for her friends if they hadn't already found her. He could keep speculating, but he didn't *know* so he walked fast and worried all the while.

Though it didn't take long to find her. The locator app led him to a hotel across the street from the one they had stayed at last night—and as he neared the entrance the screen's red bar changed to a blip. That would show him where Page was. He followed the signal into the lobby and through to a little café inside.

She was sitting alone at a small table, sipping from a cup and staring into the distance. Her head lifted and she saw him coming toward her. Her face was blank, but he knew those wheels were turning.

He rested his hand on the back of the chair opposite her. "Mind if I sit? I haven't eaten yet." He'd forgotten to eat last night as well.

Page's glance was cool. "I'm just finishing my morning tea."

"Sorry I overslept, but you got to the bank and back safely. On your own?"

She squinted. "Of course. I had the desk clerk call for a car. Door-to-door service and I was perfectly safe. Without you to protect me. Matt."

He glanced at the small gray leather bag on the chair next to her. "You've already been shopping?"

"There's a very nice little shop in that hotel you took me to. This purse is pretty, and I wanted something for a thief to steal. It's empty, of course."

Matt grinned. "*Of course.* And I'm pleased to see you're taking more precautions." Which would be his own influence on her, but he thought it better not to bring that up right now. "Still, I'll worry less once I know you've got your friends looking after you—have they not found you yet?"

"No. They've all left, even my own helpers. Last evening when we arrived, I saw your blip but no red bar to indicate that any of my colleagues exist in this time period. They've all Traveled away. By the way, this morning when I checked again, I noticed your blip and the room you'd taken down the hall."

She had known where he was this morning and could've knocked on his door, but she'd chosen this. Not only going to the bank by herself but moving to a different hotel. Now she was alone.

"Cheer up. I'm here. I'll help you find them."

Page frowned down at her empty plate. "These devices can't track each other across time. So how could we find them?"

"The old-fashioned way, research. Despite how I act, I'm no dummy. Which makes me wonder— why didn't you stay at the other hotel?"

"The old-fashioned way? I had Verity reserve a room for me here. Where I wouldn't be just a blip on the device you're still wearing."

Matt grinned. "The research may take a while. Did you think I wouldn't come looking for you?"

Page stared at him. "After you stood me up this morning, I wasn't sure what you'd do."

He caught the eye of the waitress that was floating around and signaled. He'd need to eat if he was sticking with Page. It seemed she had no objection to that, which was good, because he felt like he was still a long way from figuring her out.

Chapter 15

Destination Unknown

October 7th, 1991 The Bronx

SAM lay across the thin, hard single mattress in the cheap motel room they'd rented, and listened—to someone picking the lock on the door. They hadn't wanted to make things too easy for Kirin and who-ever she'd brought with her.

Neither had they wanted to make it impossible, which was why they'd stayed in this time instead of Traveling. They didn't want to make it difficult at all, so they'd chosen to stay here. Where Sam might make a tempting target. Though they now had the resources to stay somewhere nicer.

Kirin wouldn't know that, though. It had taken the woman three months to have her work done and convalesce and finish laying whatever plans she had for getting rid of the thorn in her side.

Which was Sam. She felt sure Kirin would want to be on hand to see the deed done, if not to commit the crime with her own hand. And according to the locator app, the woman had come.

Sam's leader device was the one that could expose Kirin's approach, and it showed she'd come in the wee hours. Probably since the woman thought Sam was alone and couldn't keep vigil while she was sleeping. She couldn't, but Bailey had.

While she had slept, he'd had the leader device and kept an eye on the locator screen to have some kind of warning when Kirin approached. When the woman had come, he'd woken Sam to let her know. Now they waited.

A faint click. Sam opened her eyes and couldn't see a thing in the dark room, but she could hear the doorknob turn and the slight swish as the opening door brushed against the rough carpet.

The night outside was dark, too. And with the drapes pulled to block out the few lights there were at this place, she could only make out the vaguest of shapes as a couple of people moved into the room. She wondered if the whites of her eyes were shining in the darkness to betray that she was awake.

The lights came on suddenly and forced her to blink and refocus. She sat up on the bed, taking in the scene before her—a grizzled man with a hairy arm filling the entrance and his arm still stretched out toward the light switch on the wall. And Kirin halfway between the door and the bed with a knife in her hand.

The woman jerked her head at the thug behind her. "Close the door and make sure we're not disturbed."

Seemingly trapping the two women in the room together, Kirin's muscle retreated outside, shutting the door as he went without a word. *Maybe she cut out his tongue.*

Sam stared for a long, drawn-out moment. The plastic surgery must've been expert indeed—even the harsh light of the motel room couldn't detract from Kirin's beauty. The woman had been restored to her old self. Unfortunately.

She only held Sam's gaze for a brief moment before flicking it around the dingy room. "Have you not accessed the trust funds yet? Or did one of the others get to this year's stipend first?"

"I told you I wasn't interested in the money. I only withdrew enough from the stipend to meet my needs. As long as you can't get your hands on the rest, I'm satisfied."

"Well, I'll have to thank you for leaving the bulk of the funds for me. Which I'll have access to once I have the leader device back."

Sam squinted at the woman. "You think I'll just give it back to you?"

Kirin sighed. "If you're smart. You offered me a deal—now I'm offering you one. Give me back the leader device. I'll keep your helper device as well so you can't track me anymore. Then I'll tell Marco to leave you alive, after he pays you back for my accident. Or I can just take what I want off your dead body. How's that for a deal?"

"You're so confident of handling me all by yourself that you left your goon outside?"

The woman bared her gleaming white teeth. "I know you don't have the killer instinct. You proved that yourself."

"And you've shown you *are* a killer. Did you really have to murder poor Harold?"

"It was more convenient that way. And if it had not been for you..."

"The only witness." Sam smiled. "I'm rather surprised you're willing to let me live. I could find a way to get a message to the others, tell them what you did. Maybe I already have."

Kirin narrowed her eyes. "I don't believe it."

"*I* believe your so-called deal is a fake. You just want to avoid a confrontation because you're afraid of me."

"Of you?" The woman gestured with the stiletto in her hand. "A gunshot might attract attention. In this kind of place, though, no one will listen to your screaming. And I want to see you bleed."

Sam's smile turned grim. "Then you should've kept Marco with you."

Kirin snorted. "I told you I'm not afraid of you."

"You should at least be afraid of the authorities. You left your fingerprints all over the knife you used to kill Harold, and the police will have them on file. Someday that will catch up to you."

"Silly Sam. I'll just make sure I have an unimpeachable alibi when the time comes. Between that and my wealth, I'll be untouchable. And you won't be around to be a witness."

"That's what I thought. That's why you've left me with no choice but to see justice done myself."

Kirin laughed. "And how do you think you can do that?"

"Well, if you must know..."

The woman's attention had been so fixed upon their conversation, she hadn't noticed Bailey slipping out of the closet. Not until he had knocked the knife out of her hand and sent it sailing across the room. Then she yelped.

The door began opening from the outside, and Bailey threw all his weight against it. Crushing the man who had started to enter into the door jamb. The thug Marco moaned. Bailey opened the door again and drove his fist into the man's stomach.

Sam started off the bed toward Kirin, then away again as the woman slashed her long, sharp fingernails at Sam's face. Bailey was busy shoving Marco into a heap in the hallway outside.

Kirin lunged at Sam again. But as Sam jerked back from the attack, the woman turned and ran for the door. She rammed into Bailey's back, pushing him through the open door and sending him stumbling over her own goon.

Kirin was a fool if she thought she could outrun Sam. The woman might've brought more help than the one thug though, so Sam didn't rush headlong after her. It might be a trap.

She ran after the woman with careful attention to her surroundings.

Kirin kept glancing behind her, and the fear on her face looked real enough, but it could have been meant to lure Sam onward. Sam chased the woman down the corridor, gaining on her all the same and following around a corner—toward the landing and the stairs down to the second floor. Kirin turned to glare as she started down the steps.

She caught her heel in the rusty metal grating and launched into the air, tumbling down one flight and bouncing over the railing.

Hurrying down the stairs, Sam leaned over the same railing and saw Kirin lying on the asphalt in the middle of an empty parking space below.

Descending the rest of the steps with less haste, Sam heard a soft moan. But when she walked over to where the woman lay and saw how half of Kirin's head was dented in, there seemed little doubt. Sam listened for last words that didn't come.

She did hear Bailey's heavy feet pounding down the stairs behind her. He stepped ahead of her and knelt down to press his fingers to Kirin's throat and shook his head.

"She's fading fast." Then he looked up at Sam, which felt strange to her. "Now she's gone."

Sam nodded and said a silent and possibly useless prayer for Kirin's soul. *Who knows what might have been in her heart at the end?* Whatever Kirin's ultimate destination, it wasn't up to Sam.

"Bailey, take the device off her wrist. Search for the other one, too. We don't want the natives discovering it." Kirin should have both her own watch and Sam's.

"We don't want them discovering us either. We should leave now." Still he took the time to remove the watch from the dead woman's wrist and hand it to Sam, then do a quick search of the body. But he didn't find the other device.

Sam glanced around at the night, but there was no one. "What if she had other hired goons? Will they come after us?" *And where in the world is that other device?*

Bailey rose to his feet and began herding Sam out of the parking lot. "Paid thugs wouldn't still be hanging around after this. After all, if they've been paid they can take their money and run—now that she's dead. Though that Marco may not be in any shape to run. Speaking of which..."

Sam nodded. They had left nothing behind in their hotel room, so she started walking fast toward the street. Bailey matched her pace, out to the sidewalk and headed for the subway. Only a few blocks away, thankfully.

It wasn't until they'd reached the steps down to the station that either of them said a word. Bailey looked to make sure no one was listening before he spoke his mind. "Now that that business is finished and we have the leader device, we can begin Traveling back to the summer of two thousand."

Sam shook her head. "It's not completely over and done with. Especially since we're not going to go looking for the others."

"What do you mean?"

She stayed quiet, listening to her heart. When they reached the platform, she led him to an empty patch of ground where they could talk undisturbed while they waited for the next train.

"We're going back to Manhattan and staying in some place a bit nicer than that dump."

"That's not what I was talking about."

"I know." Sam was still thinking about how she needed to avoid the kind of luxury Kirin had sought.

Dismissing that from her mind, she tried to decide how to explain to Bailey what she was going to do. She looked up into his face and wondered how he would take it. *Will he try to take the leader device back?*

"Something's wrong, Bailey." She turned and stared out at the empty tracks and waited until the meaningless squawking over the loudspeakers had ceased. "The way we were all scattered. Maybe the professor or someone will come looking for us, but they haven't yet. And until they do—"

More garbled metallic speech screeched from above, and Sam waited until the noise had abated. "With Harold and Kirin both dead, I'm the only one left of our research team. That makes me leader, so I'm going to make my own decisions about where to go and what to do."

Bailey stayed silent for a long moment, looking at her. "How will we know what's wrong if we don't go back? And we need to tell the others about what happened, about Harold and Kirin and us."

"That's why I said it's not over and done. Yet. If you want, I can drop you off in two thousand, and you can try to look for the others to let them know. Find Page—she's your leader. But I have another idea how to leave a message."

Bailey's blank face turned away, in thought, she hoped. Sam realized she wasn't anxious about what he'd decide to do, only curious. But as the minutes passed and the man remained quiet, she started to get annoyed.

She had other things she needed to talk about. So while he made up his mind, she talked. "I don't like the idea of keeping this extra device." *Or that there's another one on the loose.* "Since it expands the range, it'd be too dangerous to carry around. At least when I'm Traveling. I might accidentally take someone with me. The way Kirin did."

He continued to stare out into the dark.

"Bailey, I'm going to send this extra watch back to the others. If you're going to stay with me, you'll need to stick close."

He turned and nodded at her. "You're a leader now, and I'm a helper, and as you said, no one has come looking for us. So since Page isn't here to lead me, I might as well follow you."

Not as good as Sam had hoped for, but it was enough. She nodded her acceptance of his offer and turned to look down the tunnel herself as she heard a squeal and a dim rumble in the distance. Watching for the lights of the approaching train, she felt Bailey's eyes on her.

As the noise around them increased, he asked a question. "Where am I following you *to*?"

Sam turned back to him and lifted onto her toes to get closer to his ear. "The bank. I'll leave a message for Anya or Page, telling them our story. Along with the extra device." She smiled to herself. "They won't be able to eat without visiting the bank, and I can't see either of them living very long the way we have. So it should reach them."

Bailey smiled. "Certainly Page will hit the bank at her first opportunity."

Sam took a deep breath and raised her voice as the train roared into the station and screeched to a halt in front of them. "And Anya eats like a horse." She lowered her volume again. "So until someone finds us, we'll be on our own. It'll be an adventure."

"What kind of adventure?"

"I don't know, but I can't wait to find out."

Chapter 16

The Sheriff's Tale

May 26th, 2001 Chickadee County

ANYA pushed the pedals down hard, standing in the stirrups to let her weight fall and help her make it up the hill. It was so quiet in the countryside she could hear Tate breathing as he cycled behind her. A beautiful Saturday morning in May. The flowers were blooming, and the fresh, clean scent from last night's rain still hung in the air. She simply enjoyed this moment, unconcerned about the research. Or what Turner and Nye might be up to.

Both of the young people had balked at cutting their summer short, and Anya had compromised by agreeing to Travel to May of the next year—in hope of having an extra long summer ahead of them.

Chapter 16

Not too long. Anya couldn't put herself through this September, so they'd have to leave before that.

After they'd returned to the house in Chickadee, they had spent the rest of their last day in two thousand getting everything straightened and ready for their departure.

Then they'd Traveled forward to last night. And after checking around the empty property to make sure everything was alright, they'd gone to bed completely exhausted.

As soon as they were able, Turner and Nye had immediately headed back into the city to continue pursuing their own interests. This morning, Turner and Nye had been eager to catch the first train into the city. Anya had forced them to take their time over a hearty breakfast, then splurged by hiring the car and driver again to take them in.

She and Tate had lingered in silence over a second cup of coffee. Their food needed to be digested before they set off to tour the neighborhood on their bicycles. They'd be looking for signs that anything had changed while they'd been gone.

About nine months had passed for the contemporaries, and Anya wanted to know what had been going on in their lives. And in the wider world. So far they'd already visited with their nearest neighbor, a lonely widow who could usually be relied on for plenty of gossip.

Unfortunately the woman had been short with them and uninterested in chit-chat. *It must've been a rough winter for her.* While they might not have discovered much from her, it stimulated their curiosity over whether something had happened in the community to account for the woman's attitude or if hers was an isolated case.

Anya sighed. With Professor John gone, she'd started toying with the idea of taking the slow path through history. Then she wouldn't miss anything. She'd read about researchers getting too immersed in the cultures they were studying. *Going native.*

Perhaps they *should* assimilate more into the local community, become a part of the time they were studying. The professor hadn't warned them not to. It wasn't like she had much of a life to go back to in the future. Neither did Tate for that matter. He'd joined the project because his wife had passed and his children had taken over the farm.

Turner and Nye wouldn't object to living here in real time. Perhaps all four of them should sit down and discuss the possibilities—once they'd finished this summer and Traveled to two thousand two.

Anya forced herself to smile and look around at the countryside overflowing with green. It looked similar enough to the future she was used to. But there was a strange frisson to living in the past, and it energized her. *I'm in the middle of history.*

After everything that had been happening, this felt like her first chance to really take it all in—the enormity of where and when they were. Her smile started to feel genuine, and she glanced behind her to share it with Tate. His face was red as he pressed his way up the gentle slope.

It was a very long hill. Then she noticed the car in the distance, coming up the road. Anya started weaving her bike over on to the side of the road to get out of the way. She looked back and saw it was a sheriff's car.

With a vague sense of apprehension, she rolled to a stop and planted her feet on the ground. Tate came to a halt just behind her. He climbed off his bicycle and set the kickstand and came to stand at her side. *He must be feeling nervous, too.*

She hoped the driver would just pass them by, but that was unlikely here in the country. Unless it was some kind of emergency, the natives seemed to take any opportunity to stop and talk with anyone they happened to encounter. Which was good for research, but awkward for privacy.

The mud on the road had mostly dried, but not enough for the car to spin a cloud of dust behind it. Then it was slowing down as it approached, easing to a stop in the middle of the lane. *It could be anything.* They hadn't yet met the local law officers, so this was probably just a neighborly welcome.

Anyway, Anya had no reason to fear the authorities. That didn't stop her worrying, though, or the acid from churning in her stomach. She should've made the effort last year to get to know them.

At least she recognized the heavyset figure getting out of the driver's seat. The sheriff himself.

He walked around the front of his vehicle over to where she waited and tipped his hat at her. That seemed friendly enough. She was still glad to have Tate along with her, literally at her back.

She decided to take the initiative. "Good morning, Sheriff. I'm Anya—though you probably know that already. This is my friend and colleague, Tate."

"Morning, mam." The sheriff nodded at Tate and scratched his nose. "You're the people who got the old Butterfield property, right? There are more of you, I hear."

"That's right, Sheriff." She smiled at him. "But the young ones are spending some time in the city."

The man took his hat off and wiped the sweat from his brow with the sleeve of his uniform. Then he placed the wide-brimmed hat back on his balding pate. "I find that a bit strange, mam. I mean, you must've just arrived back here in Chickadee."

Anya nodded. "Last night. But you know how young people are—full of energy and impatient to expend it."

"True enough."

The sheriff flicked his gaze over her shoulder to Tate and back. "You ended your summer early last year. We tried to get a hold of you after you'd left—I don't suppose you knew that."

Anya shook her head. "What was it about?"

"We called the number you'd given for an emergency contact."

Emergency? They certainly hadn't noticed anything wrong at the house last night or this morning. "The number for our bank in the city. Were they not able to help you?"

The sheriff scratched his nose again. "Unfortunately, they didn't seem to know how to get ahold of you. I didn't talk to them myself, but they weren't too helpful. Or so I hear."

Which was no surprise. Bankers were not notorious blabbermouths anyway, but they knew little enough to tell. "I'm sorry about that, Sheriff. Anything we can do now? You never said what trouble there was."

"Well, it's kind of a long story. But it would be helpful if you could stop by for a chat. It might take a while, and it's not too comfortable out here in the heat. We might as well enjoy the air-conditioning."

"At your office? I think the weather's beautiful, but we could find the time to come around."

The man adjusted his hat. "I'd like to clear this up now if I could."

Anya thought they should cooperate as much as they could. "Go ahead and ask your questions now then. We've got the time to talk."

The sheriff smiled. "In that case, why don't you let me give you a ride wherever you're going? I can put your bikes in the trunk, and we can chat in air-conditioned comfort."

Tate started shaking his head, but Anya ignored that. "Thank you for the offer, Sheriff. But Tate can take both bikes back to the house. He has work to do." Hopefully her helper would understand what that work was without her spelling it out. "I should be able to answer all your questions."

The sheriff spared another glance for Tate and nodded. "That'll be fine."

He scratched under his bottom lip and opened the passenger side door for her. It seemed pleasant still. And Tate knew what was happening, and he'd know to get word to Turner as soon as he got back to the house. Just in case.

Anya folded her skirt under her as she slid onto the warm vinyl seat and let the sheriff close the door for her. He walked around to the driver's side and got in and put the idling car in gear. He swung the car around and headed back the way he'd come, and she looked back to stare at Tate as he receded into the distance behind them.

"I hope you don't mind going to my office."

Anya frowned. "I thought you were giving me a ride to where I was already going."

The man nodded. "Which was to my office so I could ask you a few questions. Sorry if you misunderstood."

She understood alright, and she didn't think he was sorry.

The ride into town was short, but then any trip from one point to another in Chickadee County was quick by car. Which was why she liked riding bicycles. The sheriff didn't ask her any questions while he drove, so she watched the scenery go by and held her peace.

Most of the people she saw on Main Street were strangers. The only person she recognized was Mrs. McGlinty, who stood on her front porch with arms akimbo and her apron flapping in the breeze. They all stared at Anya.

Every eye remained on her as she got out of the sheriff's car and followed the man into his office. It was a fair-sized square brick building, and inside it was mostly one big open space, with one big partitioned office at the back, a few desks lined up in the middle, and some filing cabinets along one wall.

There were also a couple of open air cells built into the wall on the other side of the room.

She walked past a deputy who was leaning back in his chair and gesturing with a pastry as he talked on the telephone and a secretary sitting at a desk in front of the office at the back. Both of them merely glanced at her as she followed the sheriff back into that office.

He nodded at the chair in front of his desk and planted himself behind it in his own rather comfortable looking chair. At least he had left the door wide open.

"Now, let's see if we can get some things cleared up." He moved some papers around on the top of his desk. "I don't know your last name. Have you got any identification on you?"

She sat and smiled. "Not on me, no."

"I'll still need your full name for the record."

"I'm just Anya."

He looked at her for a moment with wide eyes, pinching his nostrils between thumb and forefinger. "Are you refusing to give me your full name?"

Anya leaned back in the chair and considered. She couldn't tell this man the truth, that she had no family name. Yet she didn't want to lie. Leaving her with little room to maneuver.

"Yes, I suppose I am refusing. This is still a free country, I believe."

"As far as I know." The sheriff leaned back himself, lacing his fingers across his belly. "But it makes things difficult for me."

"I don't *want* to make it difficult, Sheriff."

The man nodded. "I believe that. Really, I do. So let's try some other questions."

"Let's." They were fencing, with her at a disadvantage because she didn't even know what it was he wanted. Yet.

The sheriff stared at Anya for a long minute as he rolled his tongue around in his mouth. If he was hoping she'd lose her cool, he'd be disappointed. He didn't know what she'd been through.

"For one thing, there's a little mystery we hope you can help us solve."

"I can certainly try. Who's 'we'?"

"My brothers in law enforcement. You see, last summer a man was found stabbed to death in New York City. Did you or any of your colleagues spend any time in the city around then?"

Anya nodded. If he'd talked to Mrs. McGlinty at all, he already knew that. "We all did. Could you be more specific about when exactly? Then I might be able to be more helpful." She wondered if Turner or Nye had gotten into more trouble she'd never found out about. "Was this murdered man someone I'm supposed to know? Are you saying the police suspect one of us?"

The sheriff cocked his head. "I suppose that depends on who you mean by 'us'—they have reason to believe it's one of your colleagues. One of the recipients of this Travelers' Trust business."

Anya closed her eyes for a moment. She didn't think it sounded as if she herself was under suspicion, which made it more difficult. Only one of the other team leaders had the access to be a trust recipient. *Harold or Page.* And Anya didn't have a clue what either had been up to between the time they'd landed in two thousand and then left again. Though this might explain why one of them had Traveled.

It was impossible to imagine Harold stabbing a person—anyone under any circumstances. It was all too easy to see Page killing someone in self-defense. And then running. Page *had* abandoned one of her helpers. Anya hoped Bailey was keeping the woman out of further trouble.

Until she had a better idea where this was headed, Anya wasn't prepared to volunteer information. "When I went to the bank myself, they were tight-lipped about the other recipients. I'm afraid I can't tell you much about them." Which was all true. She would have to watch her words. If she couldn't tell the truth, she'd be better off to keep her mouth shut. Whatever the consequences.

The sheriff was watching her closely. "The suspect left the knife behind with their fingerprints on it. So we know it wasn't you."

"So do I." They each had to leave their thumbprints on record when they accessed the trust funds. That would be how they knew it was one of the trust recipients, why the sheriff could say with certainty it wasn't Anya. But they had to have the name. She wondered why the man hadn't mentioned it yet.

He waited, but when Anya didn't say anything else, he continued. "We're having trouble identifying this woman. Maybe if I described her you could say which of your colleagues it might be."

"Even if you described her down to her toenails, I doubt I could help you." For a number of reasons. "But I hope justice is done."

The sheriff smiled at that. "Oh, you don't need to worry about that. We found the woman—that's where the mystery *starts*."

Anya's eyes widened by reflex, and he noticed. "I do like a good mystery. But if you already have her, I'm not sure why you want my help?"

He hesitated as if unsure how much he should say. "The prints they found on the murder weapon matched those of a woman who died ten years ago, in nineteen ninety-one. Nine years before she was supposed to have stabbed the victim."

Poor Page. "Obviously that woman couldn't be your murderer, Sheriff."

"So the New York City boys still have a mystery to solve." He pulled on his lower lip. "But if you're unable to help with that one, maybe you can with a different crime they're investigating."

"If I can, I will."

The sheriff smiled. "I'm sure you can help with this one. A traffic fatality in Midtown Manhattan. I believe it was the same day you claimed funds from this Travelers' Trust. The very same morning, just a little earlier in the day."

The professor. Anya would have to watch herself closely now. There had been a lot of witnesses to what had happened, and the police likely had a description of her. "Yes, I was there. I saw."

"No one seems quite clear how an old man suddenly ended up in front of an oncoming vehicle. Do you know anything at all about it? Or who the man was?"

John. This was becoming a minefield. "I can't help you with that either."

"For a witness to leave the scene of an accident is against the law. It would be a real problem if that person knew the victim, or was somehow involved."

Anya would have to come clean, to whatever extent she could. "I told you I saw what happened, but I didn't stick around. I couldn't explain how it happened anyway." She couldn't even begin to.

"And you can't identify the victim for us?"

"No, I'm afraid not."

The sheriff sighed. "Then you'll have a difficult time explaining your actions. Someone took a home video of you, you know. Running up to the injured man. Robbing his body. Fleeing the scene."

Anya narrowed her eyes at the man. He'd led her right into that trap—but she wouldn't have been able to avoid it even if she'd seen. "And if I knew the victim? If I had a right to whatever I'm supposed to have taken?"

The sheriff didn't look pleased. "After you've already said you couldn't identify him? He might've been already dead when you robbed him, or dying. But either way, you're in a bad spot. You can come clean about that though, and maybe avoid a charge of murder."

"I thought you knew I didn't stab that man, and what does the one have to do with the other?"

"I'm talking about this old man. On the video you can be seen taking his watch off his wrist. Anything else? And did you push him out into traffic to create the opportunity to rob him?"

Anya was aghast. She felt the color drain from her face—that she could be suspected of killing the professor. It took her a few seconds to find the calm she desperately needed.

When she was sure she could speak coherently, she did. "I didn't push him. Anything I might have taken, I had a right to. Not that you'll take my word for that."

"I'm inclined to believe you. Not that it matters what I believe. You'd be better off taking the fifth, I think."

Anya stared at him. "The fifth what?"

"I'm a pretty good judge of character, but there is the question of motive. Even without direct evidence of you pushing him, that might be enough to convict you. Circumstantially."

"Motive?"

The sheriff rubbed his index finger against his upper lip. "One of the things they were able to pry out of the people at the bank. How the trust recipients have to provide a code to access those funds. A different code each day. So you steal something off the body of this old man who dies suspiciously and then show up at the bank to claim a large amount of money from the trust. You must see what that looks like."

Anya smiled. "I can see how it might look. To a cynical mind. You're saying I stole that code, to get at that money, and that gives me a motive for murder? Is that what *you* think?"

"That's one possible interpretation."

Anya felt herself relaxing. She understood what trouble she was in, at least. "And if I can prove that I got my access to the Travelers' Trust legitimately, without any need to rob anyone? That would take away the motive. Not that it *was* murder."

"If you can prove it..."

She started to rise. "I shall. Right now, though, I'd like to go home and contact a lawyer."

The sheriff waved through the open door. "I'm afraid I can't let you leave. The New York City authorities have a material witness warrant for your arrest, and one of my deputies has already called to let them know you're here. You'll stay in our custody for now, but we'll let you call that lawyer."

He nodded at the woman who'd stepped in behind Anya. "Mrs. Salisbury here will take you into the ladies' room and search you before we put you into a cell. She's also the one who'll fix your meals—so you should hope those New York folk take plenty of time getting up here."

Anya let the woman lead her away. When they returned, the secretary handed over Anya's meager belongings—a set of keys to their home here, a few twenty-dollar bills for emergencies, her own watch and the professor's. She'd been carrying it around for sentimental reasons and now felt foolish.

Of course it immediately attracted the sheriff's attention. The man shook his head as he looked at her. "Smashed in the accident, but you took it anyway. And keep it with you?"

"Because I cared for him."

He was staring at the watch with a frown on his face when a commotion made all three of them turn to the front of the building. The sheriff was shaking his head. But Anya knew that distinguished figure coming through the door.

She didn't know how he could have gotten here so fast though, since Tate would barely have made it back to the house. Anya looked at the sheriff. "This is my lawyer, Mr. Hollingsworth."

Everyone was looking at the attorney with his salt-and-pepper mustache and expensive suit. He stared at Anya for a long minute before turning his attention to the sheriff.

"I'm afraid that's not quite accurate. I'm here representing the interests of the Travelers' Trust."

Anya shook her head. "It doesn't make any difference. I just thank God you're here."

He gave her a hard look. "Based on the allegations that have been made, there may be a conflict between the trust's interests and yours. We'll see."

Anya sighed. This kept getting more complicated. And since they'd taken away her watch, escape was no longer an option.

Chapter 17
The Slow Path

February 14th, 2001 The Upper West Side

MATT leaned back and stared up at the vast panorama of the universe above them. It never failed to awe. He didn't need to listen to the soothing narration he'd heard so many times before, but he wished he didn't have to keep shushing Page with her questions. He'd hinted at a discovery, and that had been a mistake.

He sighed and glanced to where she sat next to him in the dark. This date had been a mistake. He considered the planetarium romantic, and he'd believed Page would too, but she seemed to be bored. Since he'd seen it all before, he decided it would be better to end it now.

Matt lifted himself out of his seat and grabbed Page's hand to pull her to her feet and head for the exit. This date was only their second dud, and this time it was his fault. She'd let him decide the agenda for Valentine's Day, for the first time and likely the last. Not that he minded.

She started talking again as they were leaving the auditorium and he had to shush her again. The giant displays in the corridor didn't seem to impress her either—explaining the formation of planets and their orbits, black holes and supernovas and other astronomical phenomena. Well, he'd been forced to scrap the rest of his plans for the evening as well, so he might as well write the whole thing off. He imagined Page would.

Still, the successes far outweighed the failures. Since she'd scorned the idea of tapping into his own knowledge about dating, he'd been surprised when she'd asked for his help with her research.

She wanted to experience the rituals firsthand, and she needed someone to be the other half of the dates. So he became her partner.

With Page making detailed notes along the way, they weren't *real* dates—but they *were* a lot of fun. And he certainly didn't mind getting dressed up to the nines on Page's dime. He enjoyed the variety of the experiments as well—taking her out to a five-star restaurant and the opera one week and out to

Coney Island and pigging out on pizza the next. It had been interesting comparing a night out at the movies to a gala opening night on Broadway. Page wanted to try every kind of date.

Despite all that fun, it had also been hard work for him, since she usually demanded the full experience. The pub crawl had been an exception. Page wasn't a drinker, and she wanted to abstain anyway to maintain her scientific objectivity.

She'd tried to get Matt inebriated, but he'd had to fake it, since he didn't dare let his judgment get impaired. Not when they were out together.

He needed his wits not only to keep her out of trouble, but for another reason. It was getting harder not to sweep her up in his arms and kiss her. Or make a spontaneous declaration of his feelings.

If tonight's *date* was a dud, perhaps he'd be able to impress her in another way. Once they were past the exhibits, he drew her to a quiet place along the wide corridor to make sure no one overheard.

"You remember that website I asked you about last night?"

Page looked less than thrilled. "Yes. And I told you it has nothing to do with us. I thought you had found a lead on the other Travelers."

Perhaps he hadn't turned up much through his research so far, but it wasn't his fault. It was difficult to know if strange occurrences in history were the result of time-travelers or not, and even if they were, he couldn't be sure it wasn't future versions of himself and Page who were involved.

As for her friends or colleagues, they could even be in the future, and he had no way to research that possibility. But he *had* found something.

Matt forced a smile. "It's the fact that you know nothing about it that makes it a discovery. If it has something to do with the Travelers' Trust, and if it hadn't been set up *before* you and your colleagues were separated..."

"Then it must have been after—either the professor or Anya, I'd think."

"And if they set up that 'Travelers' Trail' website after you'd all been separated, then it *must* be for the purpose of getting you all reunited."

He thought that would make Page happy, but the look on her face was sad. She wiped that expression away, and he saw the wheels behind her eyes start to turn.

"But how can you be sure it has anything to do with the Travelers' Trust? And even if it does, how does that help? The website was incomplete, under construction. There were no details."

Matt grinned. "Not on the website itself. But I checked the registry. Now I *know* it's to do with the trust, and better yet, I think I know how it can lead us to the information we need."

Page just stared at him. "Well, what is it?"

"The website administrator is entered as Verity Dervan, that secretary from the bank that handles your people's trust."

They had just visited that bank a few weeks ago. Since none of the yearly stipend had been left in two thousand, Page had wanted to go just into the new year and get a chunk of the funds. She'd claimed a full half. They'd seen Ms. Dervan again, and she'd seemed less cross than the last time Matt had met her, but far from happy.

Matt continued. "Moreover, the contact information listed for her isn't at her workplace, but at her home. Unofficial. Does that suggest something to you?"

She shook her head. "I can understand if they didn't want to make it official through the bank, but why would they then trust Ms. Dervan?"

"Why don't we go ask her? She lives right here on the Upper West Side."

"And what about our date?"

Matt winced. "You didn't really seem to be enjoying yourself. I had planned to take you to a great Mexican place with really spicy food. And the salsa there..."

Page smiled. "I've read about the salsa dancing craze—it's on my list to try. Along with something called speed dating."

Matt felt his face flush but tried to keep his expression blank. He couldn't let Page loose on speed daters, nor test his resolve with anything as daring as salsa dancing.

"How about we save speed dating? Until we finish the slow versions? And since you said you want to try ballroom dancing, let's do that first. Though I'll have to take lessons."

Page nodded. "I've read how some couples take lessons together. We could learn how to dance, and I'd be doing research at the same time."

"That sounds perfect. But not tonight. So why don't we go and see Ms. Dervan? It should be late enough for her to be home from work, and too early for her to be eating out."

"What if she has plans for Valentine's?"

"She doesn't look the type to have an active social life, but you can never tell. Since we're close by, we might as well see if she'll talk to us."

She seemed skeptical, but she followed him out of the planetarium and down the sidewalk for a few blocks until they reached a converted brownstone. Matt pointed up at the lighted windows of an apartment on the second floor. "It matches the address on record, and she appears to be at home. Maybe she'll be glad for company."

He walked up and buzzed the intercom for the apartment and was immediately buzzed in without saying a word. He opened the door into the lobby while it was unlocked. "It looks like she's been expecting us."

They ascended the flight of stairs and had just come up to the apartment door when it swung open. Ms. Dervan stood there smiling in an elegant aquamarine evening gown. Her face fell when she saw it was them.

"What are you two doing here?"

Page stepped forward in front of Matt. "Were you expecting Turner, perhaps?"

Ms. Dervan had trouble controlling her expression for a moment, but she managed it. "I wasn't aware the trust recipients knew each other, or each other's associates."

"There's a lot you don't know. But Turner and Anya and the rest are my friends and colleagues. We need to find them."

The woman's face hardened. "Come in. They need to be found. And better if you find them first, before the police."

Matt followed Page down the short hallway and into the living room. "The police? Why would they be interested?" The other Travelers couldn't possibly attract trouble like Page.

The woman glared. "I have my own questions. Why come to me? How did you find me? And why do you think I'd be waiting for Turner?"

Page pushed Matt toward one of the utilitarian chairs. "My helper Matt here found the 'Travelers' Trail' website. And I know Turner."

Matt chimed in. "The site is registered to you at this address, but the site's not really yours, is it?"

Ms. Dervan shook her head and moved to stand behind a wooden rocker and rested her hands on its back. "It's Turner's idea, but he never got around to finishing it." She bit her lip as she looked at them. "And call me Verity."

Page lowered herself onto the sofa next to the chair Matt was sitting in. "Alright. Verity."

Matt glanced at Page before he asked the next question. "But you were helping this Turner set up the site?"

"You don't know him?"

Matt shook his head. "I only know Page. Anya and Turner and the rest are *her* friends. I just want to help her find them. Do you have any idea where to look?" *Or when?* But he couldn't ask that.

"I know exactly where to look. So do the police. The only problem is, they're not there."

Page leaned forward. "That may be more helpful than you realize. After all, the purpose of that website must be to lead us to them. The question is *when* we'll find them there."

"Turner called it a trail of breadcrumbs. They'd also put ads in various papers' classified sections."

Page's glare at Matt asked how he had missed that. She turned back to Ms. Dervan. "Neither of those things would work unless they planned to be at a particular place sometime in the future. Do you know the place? Did you ever get any hint of when they might be there?"

Verity looked at Page for a long moment, thinking. "Their address in Chickadee County is in the ads. And the last thing I heard from Turner was a message on my answering machine. Saying he'd be coming to see me next summer. This summer."

"And yet you're here waiting for him on Valentine's Day? Ready for a night out?"

"They've got a place just outside of Little Piece. It's not that far. Turner used to come into the city all the time. They talked about it as a summer retreat, but Turner never said where he would be the rest of the year."

Of course he didn't. How could he explain?

Matt glanced at Page, who nodded at him. She apparently approved him asking more questions.

"So they were planning to return to this place in the summer." Matt remembered when he and Page arrived at the end of July and her friends were gone. "But they left early last summer, didn't they? They know the cops are looking for them?"

"I don't know. The authorities didn't come to the bank asking questions until October."

Matt smiled at the woman. "And it sounds like he intended to come back this summer. At least at the time he left you that message. So let's presume he didn't know there was a problem—at least, not this one with the cops."

Ms. Dervan stepped around the rocker and sat down properly. "Yes, that makes sense. Whatever caused them to leave so abruptly, I don't know. At the time I was upset, to be left hanging like that."

Page reached her hand out to pat the woman's knee. "Men can be quite inconsiderate, can't they?" She gave Matt a look he couldn't interpret. "Until you get them well trained."

He ignored that and focused on the problem at hand. "So where do the cops come in?"

Ms. Dervan hesitated. "I hope we can help each other. That's why I'm telling you things that ought to be confidential. October wasn't the first time the authorities came asking questions about one of the trust recipients. I didn't tell Turner about that."

"Why not?" She was clearly willing to talk. *So why hadn't she trusted Turner?*

"I didn't imagine it could concern him. Sometime in July a pair of detectives came about a man who'd been stabbed to death in an alley."

Matt heard Page's quick intake of breath. He looked over at her. "Do you know something about that?"

Page nodded. "It's nothing to do with Turner. It's nothing to do with any of us anymore."

Ms. Dervan squinted at the pair of them, then continued her story. "They suspected a trust recipient and wanted to compare prints with the thumb prints we have on file at the bank. Mr. Hemmings couldn't exactly refuse, but he made them bring in an expert to make the comparison at the bank.

"They apparently matched the prints to a past recipient, who'd accessed the trust twice using different names. But since it wasn't Anya, I didn't say anything to Turner."

Matt wanted to get the conversation back onto the subject at hand. "None of that seems to explain why the cops are now looking for Anya and Turner and the rest."

"I know that. It was in October the same detectives came back with some video that had been shot at the scene of a traffic accident. We were asked if we recognized a woman in the video as the former recipient they'd matched the prints to. We couldn't. But we did recognize the woman—it was Anya, and they noticed our reactions."

Page interrupted. "And you told them all about her and this place up in Chickadee County?"

"They threatened Mr. Hemmings with obstruction of a police investigation—all he told them was her first name, and about that property."

Matt's brain was spinning as he tried to make connections. "This video had something to do with the stabbing?"

Ms. Dervan shook her head. "They implied that was the case, but what it showed was Anya rushing into traffic to the side of an old man that had been struck and killed. And then running away."

Page reached over and grabbed Matt's arm as she drew in a long, heavy breath. "Professor John. It must've been. That explains it."

She ignored the question Matt looked at her, so he turned back to Ms. Dervan. "Do you know any more about what they want with Anya?"

"No, the detectives returned and questioned us some more after they couldn't find Anya or the rest up in Chickadee County. But there was nothing we could tell them, even if we'd wanted."

"Well then, we're going to have to find out what we can about this police investigation in order to be prepared. Because I think Anya and her friends will return this summer. One problem is we don't know precisely when they might appear. But we ought to be ready to help them. Have any ideas?"

She nodded. "A young woman who's with their group, Nye, ran into a bit of trouble. I helped them get an attorney through the trust, and he's still on retainer. He can find out about the police investigation, if he doesn't already know."

Matt smiled. "Splendid."

Ms. Dervan shook her head. "There's still the problem of IDs. None of them have any. We had to buy the property up in Chickadee County for them through the trust. They couldn't even rent a car."

He looked at Page and remembered how she'd no identification on her when they met. At the time he'd assumed it had been stolen along with her bag, but now he knew why they lacked legal IDs.

"I can't imagine facing the cops without proper identification. We need to fix that. Somehow." It wasn't as if it would do any good even if they could prove who Anya and the rest really were.

Matt looked at Page and grinned. "It looks like we're going to have to get all of you fake IDs. Really good ones that can pass muster with the cops." He only knew one way for them to do that. "Do you feel like a little Traveling?"

Chapter 18

Addition and Subtraction

May 26th, 2001 Little Piece, NY

ANYA watched the iron bars swing shut in front of her, but she didn't despair. With the little cell right there out in the open, she didn't feel closed in—and with her lawyer locked in with her, she wasn't alone. He'd wanted a private word with her, and this was the best he could get.

Mr. Hollingsworth stood a foot taller next to her and had to bend down to speak softly into her ear. "One of your friends has explained to me all about those watches."

"What do you mean by that?" She couldn't imagine any of her helpers telling *all* about the devices, even to someone who was trying to help them.

The lawyer narrowed his eyes. "Another trust recipient explained how your watches can generate the code that matches what the bank has on file for any given day, providing you with access. You know this Page? That information is correct?"

Anya nodded. Remembering her previous conversation with the lawyer, she knew he didn't want her to tell him some things—and she had to judge what she needed to withhold. What it was better for him not to know. *Page is alive.*

He continued. "She showed me how to work it. All I have to do is be able to demonstrate that you can generate the code with your own watch. Then you wouldn't need the professor's and didn't have a motive for murder."

He straightened and stepped closer to the bars, calling out across the room, "Sheriff, I need to examine Miss Walker's watch."

Anya gave a small start and was grateful there was nobody else close enough to see her surprised reaction. She assumed it must have been Page that had given her a last name. She felt relieved one of the other leaders had found her, but it seemed reckless to make up a name without documentation to back it up. On the other hand, Anya couldn't imagine Mr. Hollingsworth going along with anything so dangerous. It made her even more curious to know what was going on.

The sheriff sidled over to the little cell with an evidence bag in his hand. He squinted at them both but didn't hand anything to the lawyer.

"Miss Walker?"

Hollingsworth smiled wide. "Did she neglect to give you her full name? Well, now you know."

The sheriff's expression didn't alter. "You don't happen to have any ID for the lady, do you?"

"We can get to that in a bit. First I need to verify some information about her watch."

"Surely you don't think I'm just going to hand over evidence in a criminal investigation?"

"Not while I'm standing here in this cell. If you would care to let me out?"

The sheriff grunted, but he pulled a ring of keys off his belt and unlocked the door. He stepped back and let the lawyer open the cell and close it behind him. Then the sheriff held up the bag at the lawyer and pointed at the big black letters and read them aloud. "Evidence. Says so right on the bag."

"As legal representative of an interested party, according to the allegations leveled by the authorities, I'm entitled to review the evidence. As I'm sure you're well aware. And surely you don't imagine I'd abuse my position as an officer of the court? Not that I'm conceding that Miss Walker's property *is* evidence."

"Not evidence?"

The lawyer shook his head. "While I'm sure you followed proper procedure in confiscating what she had in her possession when you took her into custody, the fact that she had something on her person doesn't automatically make it evidence.

"Considering the nature of the allegations made against her, that smashed watch *might* properly be termed evidence. But under what theory is her own watch evidence of a crime? Though it *may* be exculpatory evidence, and in that regard Miss Walker has given me permission to inspect it in my official position as a representative of the Travelers' Trust."

The sheriff snorted and stood there stubbornly for a long moment before shrugging and removing her watch from the evidence bag. He handed it over with a warning. "That's still her personal property, as you say. It's been logged in, and I'll need it back."

Mr. Hollingsworth didn't respond, he just took the watch over to hold up in front of Anya between the bars. "Now Miss Walker," he said in his clear, carrying voice, "if you'll please demonstrate for me how you produced the access code for receiving the stipend from the trust? Show me today's code."

Anya nodded and hit the buttons to bring up the account screen and generate the code. The lawyer took the watch back and compared what was on the screen with a piece of paper he pulled from his vest pocket.

He turned back to the sheriff. "I'll state for the record that the sequences match. I think you ought to see it for yourself."

Mr. Hollingsworth held the watch and the piece of paper up in front of the man and let him squint to read. Then the lawyer returned to Anya. "Since I've proven you're a legitimate trust recipient, I can now offer my services to represent you in this matter. Do you accept?"

She nodded with a smile. "Of course I welcome your assistance."

He winked at her then. "I need your formal authorization to take possession of your watch for you. Temporarily, of course."

"You have it."

"Good girl."

She ignored the patronizing tone and lowered her voice. "But what about the other watch? I don't want the authorities to keep it."

"I understand your friends have a plan to take care of that, but it's probably nothing I should know about. At least your nephew *says* he can do something. Matt?"

My nephew Matt? The lawyer must have seen the confusion on her face, but he didn't ask. "He did tell me to tell you to watch the watch." He grinned at that, but Anya didn't mind. She was busy trying to think.

The sheriff had stepped away to frown down at some paperwork on his secretary's desk. Mr. Hollingsworth backed away from the bars and walked over with a smile that seemed to have transformed somehow from personal to professional.

"If you need me to sign a receipt for her watch, I'll be happy to oblige."

The sheriff shrugged as he picked a sheet of paper off the desk and handed it to the lawyer. "As you say, it's not evidence against the lady. It seems you represent her—and if it could be an exhibit for the defense, I prefer your having the responsibility."

Anya saw Mr. Hollingsworth review the paper and take a pen from his shirt pocket. He initialed something and dashed a quick signature and gave it back to the sheriff with a handshake. "Now I'll go see what I can do about getting Miss Walker out of this mess. If you'll excuse me?"

The sheriff nodded. "But don't think you'd be able to pull the same stunt with the smashed watch. It *is* evidence, and the city boys will want it."

The lawyer walked to the door but stopped as he was pushing it open, looking back over his shoulder to where the sheriff had started to transfer the professor's device to a second evidence bag. "I suggest you keep that watch good and secure, Sheriff."

Anya stared at the door closing behind Mr. Hollingsworth for a moment before she recalled what he'd said to her earlier. Then she shifted her gaze to the sheriff. He was sealing the evidence bag, after which he made some notations on the outside and signed over the top of the seal itself.

He laid the bag on his secretary's desk and set a paperweight on top of the seal to hold it down. He lifted his eyes then to look at Anya for a moment, a neutral expression on his face.

He then handed the bag with the remainder of her possessions to Mrs. Salisbury, who tossed it in one of her desk drawers. Then he summoned the deputy who'd been hanging around, and the two of them moved into the back office, closing the door behind them. The secretary frowned at the object sitting on her desk, then started in on some paperwork. Anya stared at the watch in the bag.

Her brain was working overtime. *Who is Matt? Could it be Turner or Bailey using a different name?* She thought the plan had to be to Travel the professor's device away using her own watch or Page's, but she saw three problems with that. It might not work at all since it had been smashed. Any charge it had left would likely be minimal since she hadn't been wearing it. And it was meant to be used to generate a field through a human body and might not be able to Travel on its own regardless. She'd been afraid a device could Travel on its own when Nye was in that hospital. Now Anya worried that it couldn't.

There was also the question of where the watch might end up. If the leader device was the one generating the primary field and the professor's did actually Travel, it should suffer the same spatial displacement they'd all experienced. Finding it again would be no small feat.

Anya was wondering when the attempt would take place as she continued to stare, thinking she'd be straining her eyes a long time if it never worked, when suddenly the watch wasn't there anymore. Its blurry shape had been a visible lump in the bag and then hadn't. Thankfully no one else had noticed.

It was also a blessing she was locked up in this cell and couldn't be suspected of absconding with it. Neither could Mr. Hollingsworth, who had left before the sheriff had sealed the device away.

Not knowing what to do with herself now, Anya sat on the cot in the cell and went back to exercising her brain. Page had found Mr. Hollingsworth. *But how?* And not only that, but she'd found out about the trouble Anya was in before she knew herself, in order to send the lawyer on his way to Little Piece so early. Page must have learned what was going on at the bank.

Someone there had turned into a real talker—that Ms. Dervan, perhaps. Turner had likely headed straight for her as soon as he got into the city, and she could have passed the word to Page.

It wouldn't be surprising if Verity had lost her head over Turner, but Anya worried that her helper was losing *his* perspective. He might be confiding too much in that woman.

Anya sat and stared into space pondering Ms. Dervan and Turner, Page and Bailey, Tate and Nye, for what felt like forever. Until her train of thought was broken by Mrs. Salisbury with a tray—a nice cup of tea and some toast with butter. And jam.

Anya was just finishing the snack when Mr. Hollingsworth made his triumphal return. The man's grin was so smug it made her want to slap his face. Even if he *was* on her side.

The deputy had long since left on some errand, and the sheriff sat back behind his desk, the door to his office wide open. Her lawyer paused in the middle of the room and started speaking in what must have been his courtroom voice.

"My office has provided the New York City District Attorney with a certified birth certificate for my client. They'll soon be faxing you a copy, Sheriff. I also just had a conference call with the D.A. and the State Attorney General to arrange for a plea deal for Miss Walker. To cover her unfortunate lapse in not staying at the scene of the accident. And her failure to assist the authorities."

Anya shook her head. The man wasn't just theatrical, he was an incredible ham. 🖋

The sheriff hadn't bothered to budge from his chair and now sat squinting at the lawyer. "I'm sure you got your client a sweet deal, and I can see how you'd have demolished the suspicion of murder, but how did you get around her pilfering from the body —especially when we've got the evidence?"

Mr. Hollingsworth looked straight at the man. "It seems you were a little deceptive with my client. The video you told her about doesn't show her taking any watch, or anything else. Granted the angle makes it unclear what she might or might not have done, but where's the proof she took anything?"

The sheriff looked to Mrs. Salisbury out at her desk. "Nothing's happened to that evidence bag has it?"

The secretary shook her head. "No, it's right—"

"What?" The sheriff bounded to his feet, rushing out of his office to look for himself. Of course, they were both staring at the bag under the paperweight. The empty bag that would still be sealed.

Anya fought to keep a straight face. Particularly when her lawyer declaimed, "Have you lost something, Sheriff?"

The sheriff's smile was grim. "You're a bloody magician, Hollingsworth."

"I don't know what you're talking about." The lawyer held his arms out wide. "Search me if you'd like. Then I'd like you to release Miss Walker."

The sheriff scowled. "My secretary can swear she took a smashed watch off your client. And my deputy and I can both swear that we had it in evidence."

Mr. Hollingsworth dropped his arms. "As can I. And as an officer of the court, I'd have to. Are you sure you'd want that though, considering how you'd be at a loss to explain its disappearance? But since the New York City authorities no longer have any issue with Miss Walker, what would be the point of making an issue about this missing watch?"

"I'm not about to take your word for what they do or don't want to do about our Miss Walker."

So Anya and her lawyer had to wait while he put a call through to his law enforcement colleagues in the city. And while he waited for them to confirm it with the D.A.'s office.

Then he came and unlocked Anya's cell. "The material witness warrant out for you has been voided, and I'm told there are no charges pending and the New York detectives have no interest in coming to question you." He said it all as if would be news to her.

Mrs. Salisbury came to hand Anya her keys and her cash and made her sign a number of papers—after Mr. Hollingsworth had carefully looked them over. Which made the sheriff's face grow sour, and no wonder.

So with little fanfare Anya and her lawyer were allowed to walk out of the building and into the blue sky and its bright sunshine. And standing there by a green sports coupe were Page and Tate, waiting.

Mr. Hollingsworth turned and gave Anya a little bow. "You'll have to appear in court at a later date, when the plea is formally entered. I'll let you know when. Make sure you show up—you'll have to plead guilty to a misdemeanor and pay a big fine. But I believe that shouldn't be a hardship. Otherwise it's all over, until you get into *more* trouble."

With that last word he smiled, turned, and got into the back of his luxury sedan, then was whisked away while Anya stood there blinking in the bright sunlight. Page was still leaning back against the car she'd hired, while the poor driver baked inside.

Tate came up to Anya and took her hands in his. "As soon as I got back to the house I called Turner, but he told me that Mr. Hollingsworth was already on the way."

Anya squeezed his hands and turned to look at Page. "I hardly expected *you* to come to *my* rescue. Thank you."

"Let's save the conversation for the car." Page opened the door and slid into the passenger's seat next to the driver.

Anya got into the cramped back seat, and Tate joined her on the other side. The young driver began backing out, but Anya held her tongue and tried to decide what questions would be safe to ask. Even in front of an audience she should at least be able to find out about the others.

"Where are Turner and Nye? And Bailey?"

Page turned her head halfway. "We left Turner and Nye in the city with Verity. Your helpers would only have been in the way. As for Bailey, that story will take some time to tell."

"Tate's never in the way."

"Well, he's *my* helper, remember? As is Matt."

"Matt?"

The driver looked into the rearview mirror and flashed her a grin. "Your nephew. Although you're younger looking than what Page described. I don't know if the lawyer specified your relationship to the cops, but there may still be time to turn you into my cousin. I'd rather call you Cousin Anya."

"But who are you?"

"One of the natives you're studying. I identified your late professor as my grandfather. We'd gone back in time and established you as the daughter of one of my grandfather John's younger brothers. But we can still change that and make the professor *your* grandfather as well."

Anya was left speechless. There was too much there to really digest all at once, so she turned and looked out at the scenery rolling along.

When she was ready to ask her next question, she ignored her new cousin and shifted her focus to Page. "I presume you found out about me and the trouble I was in from that Ms. Dervan? How we'd arrived in the present from Turner?"

Page nodded. "He also told us you were carrying around the professor's device. So we needed to come up with an ad hoc plan to get it away from the authorities."

"I'm surprised you were able to manage it. The watch had been smashed, hadn't been recharged—and no one was wearing it."

"That was Matt's idea. He wore your leader device in addition to his helper watch. It increases the field strength. We weren't sure it would work, but it had to be tried."

Anya glanced again at the laughing eyes in the rearview mirror. "And is he going to search for the device now it's been Traveled who knows where?"

Page slid on a pair of sunglasses and leaned her head back. "He's had enough experience already to calculate the spatial dispersion and estimate where the professor's watch would land."

The young man held the smashed watch up in the air for Anya to see before stuffing it back into his jeans' pocket. She suddenly felt old enough to be an aunt, and she was certainly a spinster.

"You might as well leave me as your Aunt Anya."

The car was already pulling onto the dirt road that led home. Anya felt as if she'd been away for years.

Page glanced around at the property with a bit of scorn. "That Ms. Dervan you dismissed so easily helped Matt and I understand some of the things we needed to do in order to establish a really credible identity for you. For the rest of us, too. Well, we'll have to go back and take care of Tate and Nye and Turner once they decide on last names."

Matt pulled up in front of the house. He parked the car, and they all got out with much slamming of doors. A harsh sound in this quiet country.

Page nodded at Matt and Tate. "You two go on in and make yourselves comfortable. I need to talk to Anya."

The two men sauntered up the steps, and Anya confronted her junior. "So you've given that Matt a helper device and taken him Traveling. You confided in a contemporary and made him your helper."

"I exercised my prerogative. As you did appropriating *my* helper."

"The professor's death left me in charge—so I did what I needed to do."

Page stared at her for a long moment, and with those sunglasses on, Anya had no inkling what the woman was thinking. "I see you've grown attached to Tate. I'll tell you what I'll do—"

Anya interrupted. "I told you I'm in charge."

Page bared her teeth. "You have seniority, and I'm quite willing to listen to what you have to say, but you're not in charge of *me*. We're both research leaders. I have the authority to make my own decisions, and I'll do just that."

Anya forced down her initial reaction to Page's brazen assertion. Anya had been promoted to associate professor before they left and was more than just Page's senior. But that battle would need to be postponed. "So what are you going to decide?"

Page took off her sunglasses and looked at Anya. "I understand wanting a base of operations, but I'd rather work out of the city myself."

"So you're planning on sticking around and doing some actual research?"

"This is the transition to a new period of history and a lot of changes are taking place, a lot of social changes. That includes dating. Studying the changes in those customs will help me better understand the twentieth century rituals."

"I take it young Matt is going to be assisting you with your research? Why don't you take Turner as well? In exchange for Tate."

"That's just what I was going to suggest. Tate wouldn't be particularly helpful with my research."

Anya frowned as she recalled the year. "Just be sure you all get out of the city in time."

Page stared back. "And if we decide to stay and help? We can't stop what's going to happen, but we shouldn't turn our backs on their suffering."

Anya closed her eyes. "You don't know what it will be like. I've seen my share of suffering, and I'd like to spare you and the others."

There was a moment of silence, and when Anya opened her eyes again, she saw Page's face had softened. "I understand why you'd feel like that, but I still want to help with the aftermath."

They both stared at each other as they thought about what was coming. Something that never got left out of any history book. But until the time came to deal with it, they had other things to work on.

Anya sighed. "So where's Bailey? And how do we find out what happened to Harold's team?"

Instead of answering, Page drew a letter out of her bag and handed it over.

Unfolding the single sheet of paper, Anya began reading silently and realized it was from Samantha.

Dear Anya or Page,

I don't know why no one's come looking for us yet, but I know everything has gone horribly wrong. After you've read this, you'll have to decide for yourselves what you're going to do, but I've done what I needed to do.

I saw Kirin murder Harold. She took his device and fled. I couldn't let her escape justice, so Bailey and I chased her down. She was using the access to the money from the trust and the ability to Travel to make herself rich. But now she's dead, too.

That makes me a leader now. Bailey has volunteered to be my helper. (Sorry, Page, but you'll have to make do with only one. So will I.)

I'm leaving you this letter and my helper device so you can know what happened. Also that the only way we could keep following Kirin through time was because she wore Harold's device while she kept her own. Which somehow increased the size of the field for Traveling. I'm sure you'll understand that better than me, and maybe it'll be helpful. (I don't know what became of Kirin's helper device.)

Until the professor comes and says otherwise, I'll be Traveling with Bailey—who knows where or when, or to do what.

Sam

Anya re-folded the letter and stared at it in her hands. "So now there are six of us—here, at least. Without the professor's watch working, we have no way to find Sam and Bailey, and it doesn't sound as if they'll be searching for us. So much for leaving those breadcrumbs."

Page smiled. "I noticed you counted Matt."

Anya needed to reassert her authority. "You've the right to replace Bailey. And that young man of yours seems resourceful enough, so I've no objection. Now, about the professor's watch..."

"Matt is quite brilliant. Between us we may be able to repair it. Then we'd be able to find Sam and Bailey, and we could return home. If and when we want to."

Anya nodded. She'd have been better off not to carry the thing around anyway. "Alright. You can keep it. And I'll let you have Turner in exchange for keeping Tate."

Which was a better deal for her. Tate was completely reliable, but she didn't think the same could be said for Turner. Not anymore.

"That's settled, then."

Anya smiled. "One more thing. Nye will want to spend a lot of time researching in the city. You can supervise her while she's there. Of course, I'll make sure she knows to make herself available if you want her help.

Page pursed her lips, then nodded. It was done, and Anya had managed to come out well enough. If only three of them hadn't died and two weren't lost in time.

But Anya still had hope.

About the Author

JAMES LITHERLAND is a graduate of the University of South Florida who currently resides as a Virtual Hermit in the wilds of West Tennessee. He's lived in various places and done a number of jobs—he has been an office worker and done hard manual labor, worked (briefly) in the retail and service sectors, and he's been an instructor. Through all that, he's always been a writer.

He is a Christian who tries to walk the walk (and not talk much.)

CPSIA information can be obtained
at www.ICGtesting.com
Printed in the USA
LVHW041343120322
713311LV00004B/98